PIPPI ON the MISSISSIPPI™

RuNaWay GirL, RuNaWay ISLaNd

Elayna
Enjoy the
adventure!

KARI JOHNSTON

Kari John

FAIT Accompli Publishing

Pippi on the Mississippi
Runaway Girl, Runaway Island

FAIT Accompli Publishing
Phoenix, Arizona
602-466-8128

ISBN 978-0-998-58640-3 (pbk.)
ISBN 978-0-998-58641-0 (e-book)
Library of Congress Cataloging-in-Publication
data is available upon request.

Cover Design by Kari Johnston
Front cover photo © 2016 Cheri Keller Roling
Back cover photo © 2016 Janet Moreland
used with permission

10 9 8 7 6 5 4 3 2 1

First Edition

To Kenneth & Kathleen
Thank you for believing in me.

For Nathaniel & Erich
May your lives always be full of light.

Row, row, row your boat,
Gently down the stream.
Merrily, merrily, merrily, merrily,
Life is but a dream.

Contents

Author's Note

For each of us, there are places that feel important, places that are part of our past. Minnesota, the land of 10,000 lakes, is home to many of my special places.

Itasca State Park springs to mind. As little kids, my siblings and I would race along its earthen trails and teeter on rocks across the headwaters of the Mississippi River. I remember us, giddy as we selected plastic axes and Indian dolls with beaded headbands from the gift hut. Today, those trails are paved and the hut has been upgraded to a full-blown gift shop and cafe.

But for no explicable reason, the last time I was there I cried. Perhaps I imagined I might never balance over its headwaters again. Maybe it was because my earliest memories there were so fond.

The Lost Forty is another special place for me. Eighty years ago, my father was born in a lowly log cabin outside of Northome, Minnesota. During family reunions we take a day trip to the old homestead, now in total disrepair. Inevitably, we pile back into our cars and drive through a labyrinth of gravel roads to The Lost Forty, forty acres of old-growth forest the logging company forgot to clear.

In this silent, hidden place we visit a rope swing hung over a pristine lake. There, the young and the old come together to share a simple picnic, surrounded by ancient trees that block out the sun. The brave ones swing out on the rope and plunge into the freezing depths, sending ripples across the water.

There, my dad and his siblings would share childhood stories that have fired the imaginations of the younger generation, who have taken to memorizing the maze of obscure county roads so that, one day, they might return for a picnic beside the rope swing with their own children. This special place is important to our family.

In 2005 I bought a 57-foot houseboat on the Mississippi River in South St. Paul. For five years I lived year-round on the water at Castaways Marina, experiencing the good and bad of all four seasons.

When I fly home to Minnesota, I always make it a point to get down to the river. I am in awe of its beauty. Even now, I weep, thinking of the next lucky boat ride that might be offered me. The Mississippi River, on a 2,320-mile journey down the country, marks one of our nation's great birthrights.

Pippi on the Mississippi is a series of adventure stories set smack dab in the middle of Pool 2— a section of the Mississippi River that extends from the Ford Dam, between Minneapolis and St. Paul, downriver to Hastings Lock and Dam No. 2. In these books the young and the old share the unique traditions of the Mississippi River. It has become a very special place for me, and yes, I claim it as my children's and grand-children's legacy as well.

© Patrick the filmmaker / YouTube

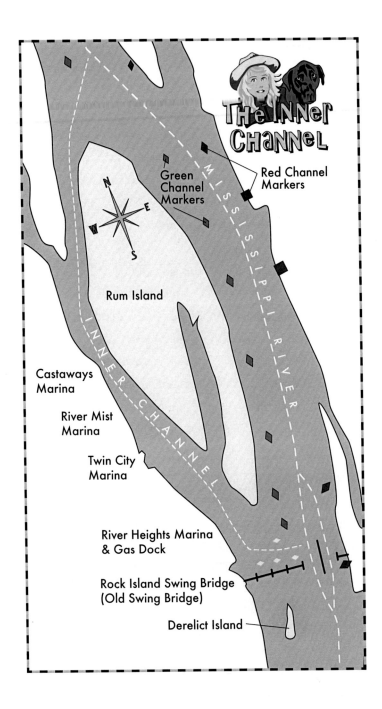

The Inner Channel

Red Channel Markers

Green Channel Markers

MISSISSIPPI RIVER

INNER CHANNEL

Rum Island

Castaways Marina

River Mist Marina

Twin City Marina

River Heights Marina & Gas Dock

Rock Island Swing Bridge (Old Swing Bridge)

Derelict Island

N
W E
S

1. The Inner Channel

GRANDPA ALWAYS SAID THAT ANYBODY CAN PILOT A HOUSEBOAT. Maybe so. I've been piloting ours since I was three.

I'm sitting on the dock at Castaways Marina having a tea party with a spider. The Mississippi River flows under us. If the spider gets swept into the river he can skirt back to the dock using web and water, but I have to wear a life jacket.

Grandpa slams the engine hatch shut and says, "There, we fixed it. Let's take her for a spin, Pipsqueak."

The men do most of the repairs on their houseboats. They spend hours arguing and sharing tools. When Grandpa finishes a repair, we take *The Karna Kathleen* out on the Mississippi for a ride.

The engines are rumbling just the way Grandpa likes, and I gather up my tea set, shoo the spider away, and climb onto our houseboat.

"Can I ring the bell?" Sometimes he holds me up to ring it, but this time he lets me stand on the Captain's chair right behind the helm.

"Ring that bell while I cast us off." The bell warns boats on the inner channel that *The Karna Kathleen* is backing out of her slip.

Then Grandpa comes back and sits me down. I can just barely see out the window. He puts my hands on the black knobs of the shifters and covers them with his big, warm fists.

"Okay, hold it steady right there while I push us out." The black knobs are used to put the engines in forward or reverse. Right now the knobs are standing straight up. The engines are idling. Grandpa hovers behind me until he's sure I understand, then slowly releases my hands.

I have the helm.

Grandpa jumps off the boat, onto the dock, and shoves on the side of the boat to guide *The Karna Kathleen* to the end of our slip without scraping his shiny new paint job. He hops back on board and returns to the helm. His hands again cover mine.

Together we pull the black knobs back and the boat backs away from the docks. With the left knob still back, we shift the right knob forward. Our boat spins left, downriver. Then we put the left knob forward too and that straightens us out as we head down the inner channel.

Now Grandpa lifts my hands off the black knobs and places them on the red knobs. The red knobs are the throttles, which make the engines go fast or slow. We nudge the engines just a little faster, but not too fast. The inner channel is a no-wake zone, which means the boat mustn't make any waves.

As we leave Castaways, going downstream, we pass River Mist Marina, Twin City Marina, and River Heights Marina. After that comes the gas dock just before the bridge.

"Ring the bell, Pipsqueak. Show them how smart your Grandpa is." He's always funny like that. Grandpa waves, bowing to his friends as we rumble by.

* * *

By the time I'm eight years old, I'm down

in the bilge helping Grandpa with the repairs. He likes the way I can jump down in there and reach all the parts on our engines. Every time I learn something new he cackles and hits his leg with his hat.

Grandpa drives us down past the gas dock, and we navigate between buoys along the bridge to leave the inner channel and enter the main shipping channel of the Mississippi River. This is where it can get scary.

We can navigate upriver to St. Paul or downriver through the Rock Island Swing Bridge. Better known as the Old Swing Bridge, it was once used by cars and trains, but nowadays the center section of the bridge is permanently swung open for river traffic. The swing arm divides the river channel in two—an upriver lane and a downriver lane.

We take the downriver lane, clearing the Old Swing Bridge.

At any time a tow might come up or down the river. The powerful towboats push barges cabled together and full of corn, soybeans, or maybe gravel. Once we're out in the main channel

Grandpa goes to the galley to get himself a cup of coffee and hands the helm over to me.

"Don't hit no barges," he always jokes.

Our houseboat was once named *Demon's Den*, but Grandpa rechristened her *The Karna Kathleen* after my mom. They say it's bad luck to rename a boat, but we don't buy into that. After all, the worst has already happened.

We never talk about the death of my parents except when Grandmother yells after Grandpa and me, "You put her in a life jacket, you hear? I'll lose no more precious children." She's talking about my mom and dad.

The Karna Kathleen is 57-feet long, and we leave her in the water year round in Minnesota. Spring, summer, fall, and winter Grandpa and I work and play on her—although Grandmother lets us live on her only during the summer.

The Karna Kathleen's hull has been re-skinned with $3/8$-inch steel and she's heavy in the water, meaning the wind doesn't grab her like a sail. Her twin 302 Ford/Mercruiser engines are set wide apart and I can turn her on a dime.

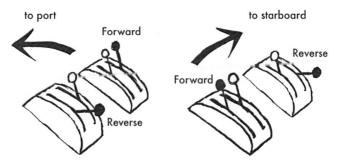

to port

Forward

Reverse

to starboard

Reverse

Forward

On a calm, quiet day with the river to ourselves, I pretend *The Karna Kathleen* is a ballerina. With the starboard (right) engine in forward and the port (left) engine in reverse, she turns to port (left). With the port engine in forward and the starboard engine in reverse, she turns to starboard. She dances in big figure eights out in the middle of the channel until Grandpa says, "That's enough, Pippi. You git a guy dizzy."

On the Upper Mississippi River we have lots of wind and chop. The helm is just inside the front sliding-glass door. When the door is wide open, the wind makes a whirling tunnel as it whips into the boat, blowing the curtains up and tossing loose books and papers into the air. My hair flies around my head while the waves pummel the bow and all manner of noises bang and bubble under our flat-bottomed steel hull. There—at the helm with the wind blowing and the waves bucking—I learn to be brave.

Most summer weekends we run three miles downriver to a cluster of islands set on the west side of the channel. Grandpa and I pull into our spot behind Island 828, named for mile marker 828 on the Mississippi River. We're 828 river miles north of the confluence of the Ohio and Mississippi rivers and only ten miles south of St. Paul.

On holiday weekends it seems like everyone from the marina is here. A quarter mile long, 828 is surrounded by sandy beaches and shady trees. We set up a campfire overlooking the main channel and watch boats and tows travel up and down the river. Grandpa knows the towboat pilots, and when he waves they blow their horns for us.

Friendly boaters pull in with their families, and we kids explore paths that snake all over the island. One trail leads to a hidden high-water lake, a hole that fills with water when the river is high. We catch bucket-loads of frogs along its boggy shores, following a stream that trickles out to the beach on the back side of the island.

On hot summer days, our favorite activity is the rope swing that's tied to an ancient tree on a sandy cliff. It's thrilling to climb the rickety ladder nailed to the tree trunk that leans out over the water. The weathered rope is tied to a branch high up in the sky and is frayed, due to all of the times it has broken off.

I've watched the older kids on the rope swing my whole life and I know to start with my right foot on the first rung of the ladder so that at the top my left foot is free to reach around to the jump-off point, a branch someone cut flat with a chainsaw. Once in position, I grab the rope above the only knot I'm tall enough to reach and swing out over the river.

Holding on tight, I wait until the rope is at its farthest reaches before letting go and falling a long way into water that's over my head. Others are not so fortunate. Afraid to let go they swing back, hit the tree, and fall down the sandy cliff into the roots. Or they let go too soon or too late and land in shallow water.

Evenings we gather at our campsite and grill hotdogs and heat cans of Pork-n-Beans among the smoldering logs while Pull-Apart Fred, Trapper, Grandpa, and others take turns telling tall tales.

* * *

By the time I'm 11, I do almost all the repairs and Grandpa sits on the dock with the spiders. For the first time he lets me pull *The Karna Kathleen* out of our slip on my own. He stands at the helm all short of breath while I cast her off from the dock. Grandpa hands the helm over to me and gets comfortable on the daybed that sits on the front deck. He lifts his hat and nods as we pass his friends, a proud gleam in his eyes.

Once we're out in the main channel, it's not long before he naps. My repairs are good, so I turn *The Karna Kathleen* toward home.

I follow a powerful tow—five barges long and three barges wide, the largest allowed in these parts—upriver to the Old Swing Bridge. Just before the bridge, the towboat slows

The W.S.Rea (front) and the Mary Jenny (top). Circa 1970

down and stops. I don't know why I decide to pass, maybe because I've never seen a tow stop here before.

I navigate the houseboat along the greens, passing the towboat on its port side. It's like changing lanes on a two-lane road to pass another car. It's not until we're almost to the bridge that I see why the tow had stopped.

Coming right at us is another 15-barge tow. This one is filled with steel and scrap metal. It's too heavy to stop and hasn't cleared the bridge yet. The towboat pilot can't avoid us.

Five blasts of its powerful horn wake Grandpa from a dead sleep. The horn screams,

"Danger! You are going to die!"

Grandpa jumps up and knocks me away from the helm. He spins *The Karna Kathleen* to port, steering us out of the channel and into shallow water near the river bank. The oncoming tow just misses us.

Grandpa navigates us back behind Derelict Island—south of the bridge and named for derelict vessels abandoned there. We see Jimi Dee's boat, tied up to a tree and half sunk in the mud. That could have been us.

In safer water, we circle and wait while both tows clear the bridge. The southbound captain blasts angry horns and shakes his fist as he goes by.

"Take us home, Pipsqueak," Grandpa growls. He has sweat on his upper lip and his face is red.

I hold out trembling hands, "I can't. I almost got us killed."

"You have to be brave to pilot a houseboat," he says. "Be brave, and smart too." He tries steadying my hands, but his fists are shakier than mine. His breathing is short, and as

I help him to his spot on the front deck his legs collapse.

"Pippi, you better git me home." He's too weak to talk after that.

"Grandpa . . . Grandpa!" He doesn't answer. Sweat runs down his forehead.

I grab the radio that only works when it wants to.

"This is *The Karna Kathleen*, over. S.O.S. This is *The Karna Kathleen*. We have an emergency. I need an ambulance at Castaways Marina, over." It takes an eternity for someone to respond.

In the meantime, I break every river rule in the book.

I use the southbound lane to go north through the bridge, cutting off a boat with my unusual course. I keep both engines in forward and steer with the wheel. I turn into the inner channel and nearly hit the buoy, leaving it bobbing in our wake.

As I approach the gas dock, I crank the wheel all the way starboard. Forget slowing down. I need to get to Castaways. Grandpa slumps over in his seat as we barely miss the gas dock.

"Hold on, Grandpa, we're almost there." I speed up, ignoring the no-wake zone of the inner channel. Boats bang, bob, and crash against docks and fenders as we race past. Angry boaters yell and captains blow their horns, but I ignore them. I have to get Grandpa to Castaways.

By now my adrenaline has kicked in and I'm frantic, trembling so much that tears stream out of my eyes. I approach Castaways just as an ambulance, lights flashing and sirens howling, pulls onto the dike wall that runs along the west bank of the river. Pull-Apart Fred is already there, standing at the end of our dock.

He sees Grandpa on deck and shakes his head.

"Slow down!" he shouts. Then his voice calmly travels across the water. "Okay, bring her in the slip easy. You've seen your Grandpa do it a hundred times."

"Straighten out your wheel," he directs. "Now put your port engine in reverse. Aim upstream, the current will help drag you back

13

downstream. That's it. Float into your spud pole. Good. Now throw me the line!" he finally shouts.

I put the engines in neutral, scoop up the line and toss it to Fred, who hitches it to a cleat. By now neighbors are here to help.

"That's it, you're tight to the pole, now pull forward."

I dock *The Karna Kathleen* in her slip and we get Grandpa loaded in the ambulance.

* * *

Grandpa's funeral is five days later. The river rats rarely socialize with the folks living up the hill from the marinas. "That's the day hell freezes over," Grandpa used to say. Yet here they are, a rag-tag band of river rats standing outside Grandmother's church, smoking and visiting with each other right up until the service begins.

Pull-Apart Fred, Captain Morgan, Scottie, Charlie, and the rest of the gang pile through the sanctified doors, wearing a hodgepodge of river hats, whiskers, and galoshes. Single file, they shuffle down the center aisle and fill the front pews—on the left.

One by one, they get up and tell river stories about Grandpa—the same stories I've heard my entire life down on the islands. Some of the men use slang words that echo through the pews. The church ladies start buzzing. But from our seats on the right, Grandmother and I sob our eyes out.

Yes, anybody can pilot a houseboat, but that was my last time piloting with Grandpa.

Nautical Terms

cast off	set a boat free from its moorings
shifters	change gear
throttles	controls the flow of fuel or power to an engine
helm	the wheel, shifters, throttles along with the entire apparatus and equipment for steering a ship
no-wake zone	designated areas where a boater must operate at the minimum speed that allows you to maintain steering and make headway
buoys	a distinctively shaped and marked float, sometimes carrying a signal or signals, anchored to mark a channel, anchorage, navigational hazard, etc., or to provide a mooring place away from the shore
towboat	a work boat that pushes barges up or down a river
barge	a large vessel used to carry commodities up or down a river
tow	a towboat with barges cabled to it

hull	The main body of a vessel minus its masts, engines, or superstructure
bilge	the lowest point of a ship's inner hull
bow	the front part of a vessel
dike wall	an embankment built to prevent the overflow of a river
starboard	The side of a ship that is on the right when one is facing forward
port	The side of a ship that is on the left when one is facing forward
along the greens	navigating on the side of the channel closest to the green channel markers
hitch	a knot used for fastening a rope to another rope or something else
cleat	a T-shaped piece of metal or wood on a boat or ship, to which lines are attached
slip	A boat slip is the portion of a pier, main pier, finger pier, or float where a boat is berthed or moored, or used for embarking or disembarking

2. GraNdMotHer & Me

EVEN THOUGH I'M ONLY 11 YEARS OLD, THE HOLY SPIRIT TALKS TO ME. Not out loud, mind you, but with "goings-on" in my head. Like when Grandpa passed, and the Holy Spirit told me I would lose Grandmother too—as if losing my parents wasn't enough. But I told the Holy Spirit, "If Grandmother goes, then I'm living on *The Karna Kathleen.*"

Grandmother grew up a landlubber in Nebraska during the Great Depression. When the Pentecostal revivals came through town, her people were converted. She married Grandpa, a lifelong river man, and he moved her to Inver Grove Heights, Minnesota. Grandpa went along with Grandmother's faith, and he called us holy rollers.

Grandmother has a scripture verse for every occasion. With Grandpa gone, my eternal salvation becomes her main concern.

She pulls my hair back in braids so tight I can barely blink my eyes. "Ouch! These braids give me a headache." *I miss my wild hair* I think, but I keep it to myself.

As far as I know, Grandmother has never cut her hair. Once a week she takes out her braids to wash long, gray hair that flows down below her knees. After it dries, she weaves it back into braids and wraps them around her head for another week.

In the mirror the high-necked dress she taught me to sew seems as foreign as my hair. "I look like a freak!" I argue.

Grandmother shakes her head and says in a long, sorrowful drone, "Vanity, vanity, *alllll* is vanity."

When school lets out for the summer, she insists I work in the gardens, weeding, harvesting, and putting up food. I invent lies to try and get out of the drudgery, but she points to the garden and says, "If anyone is not willing to work, let him not eat."

Forget rope swings and campfires with Grandmother in charge.

One Sunday after church, I slip away from our little white house, up the hill from the marina, to check on *The Karna Kathleen*, but she sees me out the window and comes running, "Penelope! You get back here. You're wearing shorts on a Sunday? You could go to hell!"

"I'm not going to hell, Grandmother! I'm going to the marina. I have to check on our houseboat. It's summertime!"

But she refuses to let me go down to the river. "Children, obey your parents."

"You're not my parent! My parents are dead. You're just an old person!" I shout.

After that she ships me off to Vacation Bible School and then to church camp where they teach us kids to harmonize to "Amazing Grace" and speak in tongues.

The preacher at Grandmother's church gives altar calls at every service. He tells us we must always be vigilant in case someone needs to be shepherded back into the fold. Reminded of the sins I want to commit, I'm always tempted to raise my hand and go forward. So it figures that church camp has altar calls twice a day.

At Lake Geneva Bible Camp in Alexandria, Minnesota, we have a morning and an evening service, but Thursday night is different. They ask, "Who wants to be filled with the Holy Spirit, with the manifestation of speaking in tongues?"

Things have to be done in a certain order.

First, you have to be saved. I was four years old when I accepted Jesus as my personal Savior.

Next, you have to get baptized by being dunked in water. Grandpa saw to that down on the island.

One Sunday morning during the river rat's version of church, Admirable Dave was playing "When the Roll Is Called Up Yonder" on his mandolin when Grandpa said, "Pippi, your grandmother wants you baptized. Go swing off that rope swing and Captain Morgan will say a few words. That oughta do it."

Captain Morgan was ordained off the Internet and she's been known to officiate at river weddings, so a baptism was easy enough. She stood waist deep in the water with her green river hat cocked on her head while I swung off the rope swing into the river. Then Captain Morgan declared, "Pippi, I baptize you in the name of the Father, the Son, and the Holy Spirit." Everyone on shore clapped and hollered.

Needless to say, Grandmother wanted me "re-baptized" in the church, but Grandpa insisted it was a legitimate baptizing—we didn't mention the rope swing.

In our church the final requirement for living a good Christian life is to speak in tongues, so at Bible camp, surrounded by other kids raised like me, I lift my hand for the altar call.

The youth pastor calls us forward and I follow the other kids down to the front. They walk us through a door back behind the pulpit that leads into the gymnasium. There we each set up our own folding metal chair in a large half circle.

Straightening his horn-rimmed glasses, an elder in a brown suit and tie stands up front and talks about the day of Pentecost, reading the scripture of how the Spirit came down on the people and they began speaking in foreign tongues. He tells us how the Holy Spirit can be called on whenever we need strength or guidance.

The mystery of such a thing and what it might mean intrigues me.

He says, "Now we're going to pray."

I'm earnest and close my eyes real tight. Colors morph behind my eyelids. Pinks change to purples that turn to gold and bright white as we're encouraged to raise our hands and worship God.

The elder instructs, "Start moving your mouth and whatever comes out is your special language."

Maybe I'm caught up in the moment, but the words I speak sound Russian.

"Praise the Lord!" he says. "She's been filled with the Holy Spirit."

With the colors flashing behind my eyelids and consonants spilling off my lips, I lift my arms toward heaven and have a mountaintop experience, communing with God.

But back at home the Holy Spirit goes quiet. I no longer speak Russian. When I close my eyes everything goes dark.

Summer turns to fall. School starts and things go back to normal, but I notice Grandmother is different.

She wants to teach me to cook, but barely has energy to hobble over to her kitchen chair and sit. Grandmother has perfected her recipes, using precise measurements and careful attention to details. All winter long, we work our way through her recipe box. She cat naps in her chair, waking up to make sure I don't miss any important steps.

Beef stroganoff, goulash, pumpkin and lemon bars, Christmas cookies, and candy fill the counters and refrigerator. Everything we don't eat goes to church potlucks or shut-ins, old people who can't get around anymore.

Until gradually, Grandmother becomes a shut-in, too.

By springtime, the church ladies—Laverne, Margaret, and Sister Anderson—alternate days watching Grandmother while I'm at my classes.

One day as I enter the house after school,

I overhear Sister Anderson, "Will Penelope's aunt come from Oregon for her or will she become a ward of the state?"

Grandmother just says, "Fear not, even the hairs of her head are all numbered."

A ward of the state? It's more serious than I thought!

Aunt Linda is my dad's sister, but as far as I can tell I've never met her. I think Grandpa and Grandmother wanted it that way. But with Grandmother slipping, surely all that will change.

I remember what I told the Holy Spirit when Grandpa passed, "If Grandmother goes, then I'm living on *The Karna Kathleen.*"

That very day a plan floods my brain and by the time spring arrives, it's well underway.

On the last week of school, Grandmother passes.

Even though I'm only 13 years old, the Holy Spirit talks to me. It gives me four words of guidance, "Tie knot. Hold on."

3. RUNAWAY GIRL

AFTER GRANDMOTHER'S FUNERAL, I FEEL MYSELF SLIP DOWN, DOWN, DOWN INTO THE DARKNESS.

Tie knot. Hold on. How?

I'm reminded of the rope swing on Island 828. I couldn't use it until I grew tall enough to reach the knot. Even then, it was the smallest knot on the rope, tied near the end where the twine had frayed.

I grasp onto an idea, a weak one at best, but maybe it's enough to let me focus on my plan. I tie my heart up in a knot and shove it out of the way, then I hold on with all my might.

My list goes like this:

1. Don't let the church ladies talk to Aunt Linda. So far, so good.

2. Move my things down to *The Karna Kathleen*. I've done most of that already, too.

3. Get away without anyone knowing. This is the tricky part.

Months before Grandmother passes, as soon as I hear I might become a ward of the state, I remove the page in Grandmother's address book with Aunt Linda's address and phone number. Then I do my best to convince Laverne, Margaret, and Sister Anderson that Grandmother and I make plans with Aunt Linda by phone.

When Laverne comes up the sidewalk to take her turn watching Grandmother, I dash to the phone and pretend to talk with Aunt Linda.

"Okay, Aunt Linda. I'll tell Margaret about that the next time she's here." I hang up.

"Hi, Laverne. I was just talking with Aunt Linda. I'm flying out to Oregon to live with her once the school year is over."

I play the same game with Margaret and Sister Anderson. Each day I make up details that reassure the ladies, convincing each of them separately that everything is under control.

I come close to being caught once.

"Can I speak with your aunt?" Sister Anderson puts her hand out, expecting me to hand her the phone.

Click. I hang up too fast. "Sorry, I think she was late for work."

Sister Anderson frowns. She looks toward Grandmother. She's resting in the hospital bed set up in the living room.

"Laverne's been talking with Aunt Linda," I outright have to lie. Laverne lives out in the country and isn't close with Margaret and Sister Anderson.

Sister Anderson looks around. "Well, what else still needs to get done?"

* * *

Part two of my plan is easier. It might seem callous that I stole rolls of five-dollar bills from old coats in Grandmother's closet. I also took food from the larder and snuck off to the houseboat while she lay in her bed at night, but I couldn't just sit in my room with my mind running wild. I had to do something.

So by day, while the church ladies help with Grandmother, I make lists of supplies I need on *The Karna Kathleen*. Then after dark, once Grandmother and I are tucked in for the night and the church ladies are back at their homes, I whip off the quilts, slip into my shoes, and rummage until my arms are full of supplies.

I sneak it all down the back alleyway and down the hill to Concord Avenue. Looking both ways for traffic, I cross the busy road to the Holiday gas station, cut through their parking lot, and follow the railroad track to the path that leads through the woods to Castaways' back door. There I hide in the shadows on the dike wall, careful that no one's around to see me hurry down the ramp to *The Karna Kathleen*.

In the dead of night, I dump load after load just inside her door. Days after Grandmother's funeral, my last bag is packed and sitting in my closet.

* * *

The third part of my plan is the part I'm not sure about. I have to find a way to take off without any of them knowing. It's also the most important. If I get caught, I'll be sent to Aunt Linda's, if she even wants me.

It's a beautiful spring morning and Laverne

waits for Margaret to relieve her, but I have it all worked out. I'd heard Margaret tell Sister Anderson that she has a doctor's appointment, but I don't tell that to Laverne. Instead I tell Sister Anderson that Laverne is staying an extra day. Now I just need to get rid of Laverne.

"What day is it?" I ask her.

Laverne answers, "It's Wednesday. I wonder where Margaret is? She should have been here by now."

"Wednesday? Oh no. I forgot to tell you! I'm supposed to walk over to Sister Anderson's today. She's watching me while Margaret has a doctor's appointment. I better run so she doesn't worry."

This better work.

"Well, no one bothered telling me. Why don't they talk to me?" Laverne huffs.

"I *am* 13 years old," I reassure her. "Did they tell you that Aunt Linda sent me an airline ticket and Grandpa's friends will be taking me to the airport first thing tomorrow morning?" I know Laverne doesn't like driving on the freeway.

"No. They didn't." She looks peeved.

"I'm sorry. That's my fault. I was supposed to tell you." *Please believe me . . .*

"Is there anything I can take care of?" She looks around the stark kitchen.

"No, it's all done for now, and Aunt Linda and I will be back this fall."

"Well, I could have stayed with you this morning if someone would have asked . . ." She sighs. "Are you all packed?"

"My laundry is done and Margaret is bringing me a suitcase," I lie.

"Well, give me a hug then. Let's say a prayer. Oh my goodness, it feels like this is all happening so fast."

She puts her arms around me. "Dear Jesus, please watch over Penelope. Be with her and guide and direct her new life with her aunt. Give her a safe trip to the airport. Amen."

Lucky for me, Grandpa's and Grandmother's friends don't run in the same circles—except that one time at Grandpa's funeral.

"Thank you for everything, Laverne." Together we walk out of the house, her to her car and me in the direction of Sister Anderson's, who lives at the end of our block. I wave good-bye to Laverne as she drives off, but as soon as she's around the corner I run back into the house and toss my bag by the door.

I call Margaret and leave a message on her answering machine. "I told you it would happen fast. My flight leaves today and I wanted to say thank you for all you've done. Grandpa's friends just got here and they're taking me to the airport." I repeat what I said to Laverne, "Thank you for everything." *Lord, please forgive me.*

Finally, I work up my nerve and call Sister Anderson.

She answers on the first ring. *Oh no.*

"Sister Anderson? This is Penelope. I want you to know that Grandpa's friends are here to take me to the airport. It's happening as quick as we thought it would. I fly out today so I wanted to say thank you for all you did to help us."

"I'll come right over," Click. She hangs up the phone.

I have to leave now!

I grab the bag, lock the door, and run to the purple lilacs that line the back alleyway. I dive into their hidden tunnels, my heart throbbing. The knot slips.

For years the lilacs were my secret hide-out. Now in full bloom, the thick hedge hides me from sight. I peer out and notice the picnic table, my ship for adventures on the high seas. The table needs a fresh coat of stain. Underneath it new blades of grass poke up between leaves forgotten last fall.

Sister Anderson arrives and knocks on the side door of our house. No answer. She raps on a window, "Penelope, are you still here?" She takes a deep breath, clasps her hands together, then looks up. "Well, she's gone, just like that." she says to the sky.

She walks around our yard, looking at Grandmother's gardens that need to be plowed under and planted. Sister Anderson stops by a pink, ruffled peony—at full bloom in the center of an old tire, once painted white but now grey from age and weather.

She reaches for the stem and tries to break it off, but it's too tough and after working the sinewy branch back and forth and back and forth, she gives up.

How sad she looks as she walks back to her home up the street, leaving the flower hanging from its broken limb.

It's a quiet gut punch.

What have I done?

All I can smell is lilacs, reminding me of Grandmother. I feel like throwing up.

The knot slips loose from my heart, but the coast is clear.

I crawl out of the lilacs, run down the back alley, across Concord Avenue, through the Holiday gas station parking lot, and along the railroad tracks. When I get to the woods I follow my well-worn trail and arrive at Castaways Marina in a blur of tears and snot.

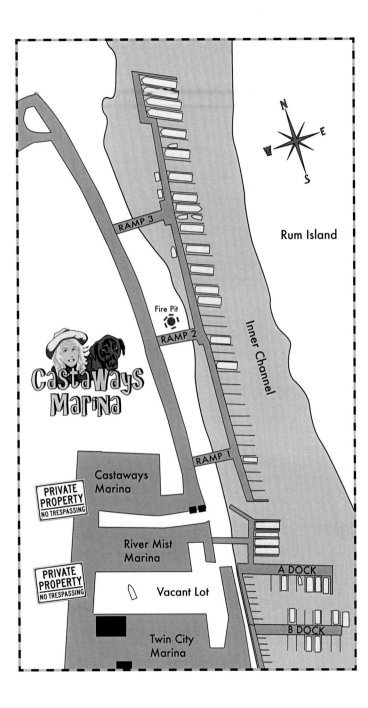

4. Castaways Marina

Each hole in the water at Castaways has a private owner. The tidy row of 42 slips is lined up against the main dock that runs parallel with the shore. The entire marina is pinned in place by massive spud poles, pounded deep into the river bottom. The spud poles support docks that float up and down the poles as the water levels rise and fall.

Today, half of the holes are filled with live-aboard boats. These hearty folks have endured another brutal winter on the Mississippi River in Minnesota. If the weather cooperates, the summer boaters will pack the marina by Memorial Day with every type of riverboat imaginable—houseboats, cruisers, pontoons, muscle boats, canoes, and maybe even a paddlewheel boat.

Ramps 1, 2, and 3 cross the water from the dike wall down to the long dock. I'm hiding in a sunny patch of wild honeysuckle on the dike by Ramp 3, the farthest north and the most isolated.

Using my sleeve, I wipe my face but the silent tears won't stop. None of my body parts feels connected. By accident my shaky knees keep hitting each other. My heart is pounding—bump, bump, bump—like the semitrucks I hear driving across the Wakota Bridge, one river mile north of here.

The mix of sun and tears makes the bruises on my bony shins reflect the colors of the rainbow. I don't know where they all came from. I press down on the biggest bruise. It hurts, so I push on it again.

Running away was a terrible mistake. *Maybe I should go back.* Then I look at our houseboat.

The Karna Kathleen berths with the larger boats on the north end of Castaways. Peering through honeysuckle vines, I see her. I don't remember her light blue siding and deck ever looking this dirty. She looks as sad and abandoned as I feel. I know Grandpa's friends have done their best, but keeping up a houseboat on the Mississippi is a lot of work.

The Mississippi River starts as a trickle at Itasca State Park in northern Minnesota. As it winds south, streams and tributaries fill it with snowmelt and runoff. The trickle grows into an impressive river by the time it has traveled 500 miles to Minneapolis and is joined by the Minnesota River before it flows through St. Paul, eight miles north of here.

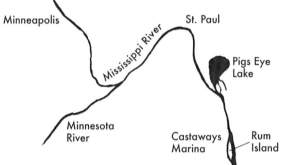

As the river approaches Castaways, it splits around Rum Island—a long island that protects Castaways and three other marinas from wind and waves. The island creates an inner channel on the west side of the river.

Towboats strapped with barges come down from Pigs Eye Lake and points north, navigating between green and red channel markers on the other side of the island. At Castaways the inner channel, Rum Island, and the main river combined are almost a quarter mile wide.

When the river runs high, deadheads—fallen trees, logs, and stumps—pile up on the northern tip of Rum Island. The fear is that the deadheads will build up and eventually block the inner channel, so once a year boaters clear the logjam. It's just my luck that today is that day.

Grandpa used to say, "Castaways has the most dignified gossips on the Upper Mississippi River." It will be impossible to sneak aboard *The Karna Kathleen*.

What was I thinking? That I could just waltz onto her and no one would notice?

Trees the size of small houses float past as the men in boats pry them loose and release them downriver. This is a terrible time to sit sulking in the bushes. Forget about running back to Grandmother's house. Seeing the condition of *The Karna Kathleen*, I know my boat needs me.

Distracted by river life, my tears stop.

I crawl out of the bushes and run down Ramp 3 that crosses from the shore to the main dock. The ramp bounces as the water rushes beneath it. The main dock runs in front of *The Karna Kathleen*. On both sides of her are narrower docks, called *fingers*. Heavy metal cleats attached to the fingers support thick lines that hold the houseboat in place.

I toss my bag aboard, yank my life jacket from the front hook, and run down the port finger to her stern. I try shrugging into the vest but it has shrunk, or I have grown. I sling it over my shoulder anyway and race to the back of my boat. The huge deadheads floating past us could be dangerous if they collide with the dock or hit a boat.

As dockmaster at Castaways, Pull-Apart Fred is in charge of clearing the deadheads off the tip of Rum Island. Fred has lived most of his life with an artificial leg, an artificial arm, which he seldom wears, and several fingers blown off his remaining hand—the result of a horrible event when he was a young Marine serving in Vietnam. I once heard him tell how he lay there in shock after the explosion, looking at his separated limbs, and all he could say was, "Oh sh∗t."

Fred sports a contagious personality, sometimes exaggerated by beer, and got his nickname Pull-Apart—river rumor goes—when he lost his balance and fell into the river. His friends tried pulling him out, but instead pulled off his artificial arm. They tried again but then pulled off his artificial leg. It took the whole gang to haul him out, and he's been called Pull-Apart Fred ever since.

Pull-Apart and his best friend, Davy, are in Fred's jon boat, a shallow flat bottom workboat. One handed, Pull-Apart drives it right up on the tangled pile of deadheads. Sometimes Davy fires up his chainsaw to hack away sections of tangled logs and limbs. Sometimes they throw a towline over a log and Fred pulls it free with his boat, dismantling the logjam one piece at a time.

The result is impressive. Once stately trees, with long branches and newly sprouted leaves, now float past with roots exposed to the sky.

The barrage of timber, logs, and debris hits Castaways first. My neighbors wave to me as we stand on the end of our boats, using long poles with hooks to push the logs on down the river.

"It's huge! Do you need help?" or, "Wow! Try pushing it again," we call out, working together.

Today, getting the deadheads past Castaways becomes my sole purpose in life. I am armed with an impressive pole. Unlike the aluminum hooks sold at the boating supply store, Grandpa made our pole out of ten-foot-long steel pipe, capped off with a blunt, metal spear.

Wary neighbors stand back as I run up one finger to the main dock and then down the next finger, waving my oversized weapon, my life jacket flapping in the wind. The long pole is heavy and more than once my spear hits a spud pole and I risk falling into the water before pushing a heavy log away from the boats.

Different folks have different ideas of what constitutes a sin. At Castaways Marina, letting a log get jammed under a dock to become a permanent fixture is considered a major sin. We all work together to prevent this.

All eyes are on the logs and debris floating past when we hear Fred and Davy yelling. While Fred was using the front of his jon boat to bump deadheads from the top of the island, a huge tree snagged his propeller. The next sound traveling across the water is Fred's engine clicking. His motor is dead.

The fast current takes over and the tree, wedged under Pull-Apart's engine, pushes them down the inner channel.

The two men know that a sideways boat on a rushing river can be perilous, so they fight to keep the boat pointed south. Fred uses his ample girth to trim the bow, shifting his weight forward, while Davy bounces up and down in an attempt to lift them off the enormous limb.

Wide-eyed, we watch helplessly as Fred and Davy try prying their engine loose from the most enormous tree I have ever seen in the water. The tree and the jon boat are rushing headlong toward Castaways, aimed directly at *The Karna Kathleen*!

Pull-Apart hollers, "Hold on, Davy!" as the boat lists dangerously to port.

The look on Fred's face is one of sheer terror as the jon boat hurtles towards me. There is no way for him to escape a collision.

The impact is brutal. Fred falls off of his seat and lands in the bottom of the boat, and Davy barely saves himself from being dumped into the ice-cold water by clinging to the gunwale.

I step back as the jon boat hits hard and scrapes along *The Karna Kathleen's* steel hull before it veers back out into the inner channel, the log still pushing them from behind. That's when I notice the line tied to a stern cleat on my boat.

I pick that exact moment—when Fred is trying to hoist his body, one-handed, back up on the seat—to throw the line and yell, "Fred, catch!"

The line completely misses him, and he shoots me a dirty look. But Davy picks himself up off the floor of the boat, snakes his arm out, and snags the line. In no time flat, he ties a bowline knot around a thick branch of the tree they're stuck on.

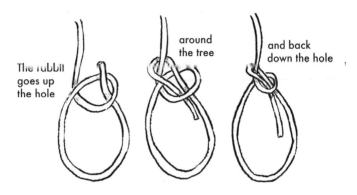

The rabbit goes up the hole

around the tree

and back down the hole

Bowline Knot One of the most useful knots on a boat.

It feels like forever before the rope reaches its full length, stretches, tightens, and finally —to everyone's relief—holds. My heavy boat is jerked and tugged, but sure enough, the log halts.

Pull-Apart's boat pulls free from the log, which is now tied-off to my stern cleat.

The men inspect the prop, then fire up their engine. True to his nature, Fred shows off, cutting a swath through the water with his jon boat.

"Hey Pippi, good thinking!" he hollers loud enough for half the marina to hear.

He takes a moment to let the crowd whoop and bark comments, then pulls up behind *The Karna Kathleen* to strap a line around the tree and haul it downriver.

"Is school out already?" he asks.

Using his stump, he raises his shirt to his face and wipes away sweat, exposing his big belly. I try not to look.

Then, out of the blue, I bluff. "Yes, and guess what? I get to spend the summer on my boat." *Did I just say that?*

Fred responds, "Well, the first thing we better do is find you a decent life jacket, especially if you're gonna be down here lassoing hundred-foot-long trees!" He knows Grandmother's rule. "Come over for lunch today, and we'll have Lu find something that fits."

"Sounds good, thanks." Lunch on Fred's boat reminds me of old times, but then I remember Lu.

Oh, sand fleas! Lu is going to grill me, but I made a deal with the Holy Spirit and that means I'm back home at Castaways. So, with the inner channel cleared, and the last of the deadheads floating south, I board *The Karna Kathleen*, this time as Captain.

Nautical Terms

spud pole	a pole pounded into the river bottom that docks or boats can be attached to and allowed to rise or fall as the water level dictates
live-aboard	Someone who makes a boat, typically a small yacht or houseboat in a marina, their primary residence
berth	the space allotted to a vessel to anchor or tie up, to bring to, or install in a berth, anchorage, or moorage
green channel marker	marks the edge of the channel on your port (left) side as you enter from open sea or head upstream
red channel marker	marks the edge of the channel on your starboard (right) side as you enter from open sea or head upstream
deadhead	a sunken or partially submerged log
finger	an object that has roughly the long, narrow shape of a finger, docks sticking out from a main dock
line	once a rope is on a boat, it becomes a line
dockmaster	someone in charge of the day-to-day maintenance of a marina, often helped by an assistant dockmaster
jon boat	a flat-bottomed boat capable of operating in extremely shallow water with a transom to mount an outboard
boat hook	An aluminum pole with a hook on one end commonly used to aid docking and undocking, or for pulling things out of water, such as debris or people, as well as for other fetching tasks.

head of an island	the upriver end of an island
top of an island	the upriver end of an island
foot of an island	the downriver end of an island
tail of an island	the downriver end of an island
bottom of an island	the downriver end of an island
current	a steady and continuous flowing movement of some of the water in a river
trim the bow	to even out a keel fore and aft
gunwale	the top edge of the side of a boat
bowline knot	a nonslip loop on the end of a rope

The Karma Kathleen

Main Level

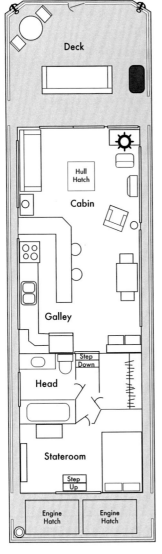

Deck

Hull Hatch

Cabin

Galley

Head

Step Down

Stateroom

Step Up

Engine Hatch

Engine Hatch

Upper Deck

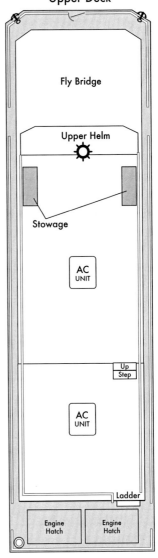

Fly Bridge

Upper Helm

Stowage

AC UNIT

Up Step

AC UNIT

Ladder

Engine Hatch

Engine Hatch

5. Haunted Houseboat

GRANDPA'S GHOST LIES JUST INSIDE *THE KARNA KATHLEEN,* SO I HANG OUT ON THE FRONT DECK LOOKING AROUND.

After two neglectful years, the deck is a mess. The daybed hogs up most of the space. A small patio table is pushed to one corner and its chairs are folded up, lying on their sides. The grill is shoved against a pile of anchors, dirty lines, and an old bucket.

Each fall the community comes together to shrink wrap our houseboats. Snow and ice slide off the plastic into the river—instead of weighing down the boats and possibly sinking them.

Grandpa and I built a structure out of two-by-fours that covered our boat, and with the help of friends pulled a giant sheet of plastic over the entire structure, deck and all. Then Howie would come by and shrink the plastic tight with his heat gun. Howie's crew has done all this work since Grandpa's death.

When they removed the shrink wrap this spring, scraps of white plastic, wood lath, and bent nails were left strewn across the open deck. Dirt, mold, and leaves now add to the disarray, and the once fluffy rag rug in front of the sliding glass door looks like road kill. I start there.

I pry the rug, stiff with rigor mortis, off the deck and throw it onto the dock. As I move stuff around I find a broom behind the daybed. I dip its bristles in the river, and use it to swab the deck.

How should I arrange my new home?

In my fantasy, I live happily ever after on my beautiful boat. Friendly spiders, so large they have names and personalities, crawl out from under the dock to look for prey and stop in for a spot of tea. Randy ducks frolic all over the marina, quacking and snagging bits of food from the water. Eagles soar overhead, showing their oversized, black-headed babies how to catch fish.

Grandpa's friends, stopping by to check on *The Karna Kathleen*, must have used the shrink wrapped deck to get out of the weather and find protection from the elements. I notice the daybed has been turned around, facing in, and the old ashtray is full of butts.

Built of logs, the daybed looks like it should be in a log cabin—except that the thick cushion is upholstered with heavy duty fabric decorated with sailboats, seagulls, and boating insignia. With the shrink wrap gone and the deck open to the world, I shove the daybed back around to face out and leave a lane behind it so I can board from either side of the boat.

Already, my boat feels friendlier. I like to sit on the daybed and watch the comings and goings up and down Ramp 3. People walk past on the dock and sometimes stop to visit.

The real benefits of a forward-facing daybed come when *The Karna Kathleen* is out on the river. At full throttle I can sit and watch the waves rush toward us. When we anchored out, Grandpa would let me sleep out on its thick mattress, gently bobbing between twinkling stars and shimmering water.

With the daybed back in its place, I set up the small table and chairs to create a pleasant sitting area, swabbing as I go. I roll the grill to one side, and hang up the anchors and lines on their hooks so they'll be river-ready. Satisfied, I direct my gaze toward the front door.

The ancient screen door is kittywampus. One wheel of the rolling door hangs off its track.

That won't do.

The state of our houseboat would humiliate Grandpa if he could see it. The light blue siding on the main cabin is caked with grime.

I go to the stern of *The Karna Kathleen*, walk across the large engine hatches, and climb the ladder to the upper deck. Dark green mold covers the once light blue carpeting. I find a flat screwdriver in the tool bin beneath the upper helm.

Topside the wind picks up and blows across my face. The sun darts behind fast-moving clouds. From here I get a bird's-eye view up and down the river. North, past Rum Island, parts of the Wakota Bridge are visible through the sprouting trees on the island and river bank. It won't be long before their new leaves fill in and Castaways becomes completely hidden from the outside world. I can hardly wait.

I back down the ladder and hop onto the metal engine hatches. They're streaked with rust. As I walk back along the side rails I can almost hear the rust munch furiously on places where the paint has chipped. The metal needs to be sanded, primed, and painted. Grandpa would be appalled. Two years of neglect is an eternity for a boat.

Back at the screen door, I get to work with the screwdriver. I pry the wheel back onto its track and test the door.

When I roll it open I hear Grandpa's cheerful voice echo out of the past, "Close the screen door! You're letting in mosquitoes . . ."

Chills run down my spine. *He's here.*

I slide open the glass door, centered on the front of the boat. I part the long, thick drapes and step into the darkened cabin.

Once inside, I pull the cord and open the

drapes, flooding the entire room with light. Behold, a total and utter mess of my own making is spread out before me.

Over the last month I had collected supplies while making plans to escape. After dark, I made secret trips to my boat, hauling quilts, blankets, bedding, clothing, and books down the back way from Grandmother's house to Castaways.

Grandmother and I had canned food from her gardens, so night after night I raided our pantry for jars of applesauce and apple butter, tomatoes, beans, peaches, and corn, along with cans of Spam and tuna. On my last trip I snatched Grandmother's recipe box from the kitchen counter and brought it down to *The Karna Kathleen*.

Today, my secret bounty is scattered all over the cabin floor. I pick my way through the piles and come to the recipe box lying on its side. I reach down and pick up the small wooden box and the tears start flowing.

What was I thinking?

The boat looks derelict to people walking

by and I have endless days of hard work ahead.

Grandmother's house has small, tidy rooms packed with knick-knacks and crocheted doilies, but *The Karna Kathleen* is 57 feet long and every wall is filled with windows or glass doors.

The starboard side of the cabin features the helm and Captain's chair. A small television—that only works if the rabbit-ears antenna is pointed in the correct direction—sits in front of Grandpa's recliner and a reading lamp.

Past the recliner, in the dining area, a table and two chairs sit in front of a second sliding glass door. It's a curious place for a door. The story goes that the previous owners were anchored out. In the dead of night, a boat drove right into the main cabin. The wife ended up liking the added light and insisted that the wall be replaced by a patio door.

The back wall of the dining area holds the washer and dryer with cabinets above them for cleaning supplies.

The port side of the cabin, across from the helm, has an oversized sofa, once considered my bed. Beyond that, an island curves around the galley, which takes up the rest of the room.

By boat standards, our galley is gigantic—it's big enough to be a kitchen in a small house. Soft yellow curtains, sewn by Grandmother long ago, when she used to come down to the river, make the whole cabin feel homey.

Centered steps lead down to a short hallway. The head—with a tub, toilet, and vanity—features framed prints of dogs playing poker. Across from that, a large closet holds more tools, winter coats, and the house battery that powers the macerator toilet and the water pump. The sewage and water tanks are stored down in the hull.

The main stateroom takes up the back end of the boat. It holds Grandpa's bed, dresser, and bookshelf. Steps lead up and out the aft door to the metal engine hatches, and when we are out on the river the curtains fly out, following us down the river.

I can't stop the tears from flowing, but that doesn't mean I'll do nothing. I set the recipe box on the galley island and pull my shoulders back. Before going to Pull-Apart Fred's I have a couple of chores to get done. Besides, it's never a good idea to arrive at an inquisition early.

First, I need to change into river clothes. Digging through my bags, I find jeans and a T-shirt, tennis shoes, and a jacket. Toward the end of her life, Grandmother had me in dresses almost seven days a week. I go into the head and change, throwing my dress in the corner. I won't be wearing that again anytime soon. My hair is pulled into two tight braids. I unroll the rubber bands and pull the braids loose. Blonde hair spills free and frames my face, now streaked with dirt from the bushes. I stare into serious blue eyes. I look and look at them, but they don't have any answers. I blow my nose, dusted with sun freckles, wipe away the smudges, and get to work.

Mounted outside on the front of our slip are the water spigot, electrical box, and cable TV connection. I open the lid of the electrical box and flip both breakers on.

Inside the cabin I step over the mess and grab a flashlight. I hunt for the breakers under the helm and lift the inside breakers to ON. I flip the light switch. Nothing. The electricity isn't working.

Getting down on my hands and knees, I shine the flashlight into the panel. Both of the breakers are in the ON position.

Back out on the dock I also confirm that the outside breakers are on.

I inspect the large yellow power cords. Both are tightly screwed into the electrical box on the dock, and their outside mounts on the boat.

Back inside, panic rises in me. The helm is packed with knobs and switches that I've never noticed before. None seem to have anything to do with the power.

I go through the boat flipping on all the switches. Again, nothing.

Grandpa, is this your doing?

I walk through each room, opening all the curtains and mini-blinds. Sunshine floods the boat from the south windows, only emphasizing my mess.

I need power. Minnesota gets cold in May.

The blower on my heater won't work. Neither will the lights or the refrigerator. Under these conditions no one will let me stay here.

I pull the cord and close the front drapes, hiding my mess from passers-by. I head down the dock to Pull-Apart Fred's boat and to an inquisition that will decide whether I'm kicked out of Castaways or not. I straighten up my shoulders and act like everything is fine.

Nautical Terms

board	to get onto
anchor	a heavy object attached to a rope or chain and used to moor a vessel to the sea bottom, typically one having a metal shank with a ring at one end for the rope and a pair of curved and/or barbed flukes at the other
shrink wrap	to cover your boat with a heavy plastic to protect it from the effects of the elements
heat gun	used to heat and shrink heavy plastic over a boat for protection
swab the deck	mopping the deck
stern	the rearmost part of a ship or boat. Also called rear (end), back, after end, poop, transom, tail
upper deck	roof of a houseboat reinforced for use
helm	a lever or wheel controlling the rudder of a ship for steering

upper helm	the helm located on the upper deck
topside	the upper deck
derelict	doomed or lost. very poor condition as a result of disuse and neglect
cabin	the main room serving as an assembly room on a boat
galley	a kitchen on a boat or ship
head	a bathroom or toilet, especially on a boat or ship
stateroom	a private room on a vessel

6. Secrets & Lies

I DON'T BELIEVE FOR ONE MINUTE THAT FRED INVITED ME TO LUNCH BECAUSE OF MY LIFE JACKET. He wants to know what I'm up to, and he knows Lu will grill me. Lu has four grown kids scattered across the country and she took to mothering me a long time ago.

Usually breakfast for lunch is my favorite meal, but today I dread it. I step aboard the *Credenza,* Fred's 52-foot WaterCraft houseboat, and knock on the glass door.

"Come in!"

Pull-Apart's vessel is in tip-top condition. One side of the cabin has the helm and the television. A small galley kitchen is on the same wall. Lu has the electric fry pan plugged in and the smell of bacon fills the boat.

On the other side of the room Fred occupies the sofa watching *The News at Noon.*

"Hi, kid." He waves absently, dismissing

61

me. It's almost as if he's forgotten he was in a boat wreck a couple of hours ago.

Beyond the sofa is a table, already set for three. Stairs in the middle of the back wall lead down to the stateroom and head. Sun streams into the custom-draped windows, emphasizing the smoke that rises from cigarettes in two separate ashtrays. My eyes start to burn.

Lu saves the real business for later. For now, she puts me to work toasting white Wonder Bread and spreading it with Land-O-Lakes butter while she fries thick slices of bacon in the pan.

Lu talks about her kids—John, Lysa Marie, Terry, and Jerry—and I watch her chest puff out, her eyes twinkle, and love shoot out from her heart through the gap in her front teeth. I wonder if my mother ever had such a look on her face.

I think she can tell I've been crying. To distract me she talks about her son's new dog, Leo. Lu can't talk without using her hands. In one she holds the tongs, turning the hot bacon between gestures, and in the other she holds her cigarette.

I step back as Lu describes the dog's white patch on his chest. I watch the hot tongs and cigarette. She waves her cigarette hand. Fred and I notice an ash fly off into the sizzling bacon. He clears his throat, but then just shrugs.

When you see Lu's eyes sparkle, you know there is a God. You also know you're not going to get a word in edgewise, which suits me just fine. But just in case, I ask her to remind me how many grandchildren she has. Fred rolls his eyes at me.

Lunch is a solemn occasion served with the precision and respect due a Marine. Lu pulls out a chair for Fred, formally inviting him to join us, even though he's in the same room. He puts out his cigarette and comes to the table. Lu brings her ashtray from the galley, her cigarette still burning. Its smoke makes squiggly ghosts that drift toward me through the sunbeams.

Careful orchestration follows. To the blare of the news, Fred takes a piece of toast from the neat pile. I'm used to seeing his hand with only two and a half fingers do anything a regular hand can do. He lays the toast on his plate. Lu walks his plate to the fry pan, lays an over-easy egg on the toast, and returns the plate to Fred.

Fred takes his battery-powered salt and pepper grinder, seasons the egg by pressing buttons, and piles bacon on top. One-handed, he folds the bread into a messy half-sandwich, and begins eating.

Next, Lu serves the two of us. She sits down and finally grinds out her cigarette into the ashtray.

I pick at the edges of my food—refusing more when Lu serves up seconds and thirds to Fred. I focus on the television news and try not to watch him eat.

Fred signals he's full by sitting back and patting his stomach, so Lu gets up and hands him a clean, wet washcloth. He lays his hand on it, wiping away the bacon grease, then puts the cloth to his face, picking yolk from his neatly trimmed beard and mustache, cleaning his face like a cat using his paw in the sun.

Then Fred goes down the steps to the head and comes back, retiring to the sofa. There, he takes off his leg and lights a cigarette.

I wash dishes while Lu picks up, tucking the table back against the cabin wall. When she is finished, she shoves me out of the way and washes the greasy fry pan. By the time we're done, Fred is snoring on the sofa. So goes a typical noonday meal on Pull-Apart's boat.

Lu and I go through life jackets, finding one that fits me, and then she directs me to sit down. She fills a glass with ice and pours vodka and Clamato juice over it, offering me a Coke. She lights a cigarette. The inquisition begins.

"Now, who's watching you?"

"Well, my dad's sister, Aunt Linda, is working with me." I fiddle with the pocket of Grandpa's flannel shirt.

"Have *I* met your Aunt Linda?" She pulls a drag off her cigarette, squinting one eye as she blows smoke to the side.

I haven't even met her so, no, I don't think you have.

"No, she's never been to Minnesota," I

inform Lu.

"Oh, so you're *working* with her? How? By phone?"

I'm trapped already.

"Yes, that's right." Judging by her look, it doesn't fly. "But she's coming to Minnesota," I add.

"Oh, I see. When is she getting here?"

"Actually, she's on her way." This is becoming a problem. Jaws wag in a marina. Down here there are no secrets. I adjust, "She's moving into Grandmother's house up the hill. She'll come down to the marina on weekends . . . or, I'll go up to the house and see her . . . it's just for the summer," I hope this makes sense. *Can I get in any deeper? Why can't I just take care of myself? Do these people think I'm helpless?*

"Well, I'm really looking forward to meeting her." Lu knocks an ash off her cigarette and takes another drag.

The boat leans to one side. We have company. I breathe a sigh of relief. For now, the inquisition is over, but what have I done? I'm

66

in shock and sit there stone-faced.

Three members of the Castaways' board of directors arrive for an off-the-cuff meeting. As dockmaster, Fred holds court from his sofa where he now sits with his naked stump exposed and his prosthetic leg leaning against the wall. The day-to-day business of running a marina never ends.

"Grab a beer," Fred hollers as he wakes up.

The men help themselves to the cooler out on the front deck while Lu sets up chairs.

Fred asks, "Pippi, will you grab some beers from the cooler for me?"

I am fully trained in Fred's beer protocol. His little beer cooler holds six beers. I fill it with ice-cold beer from the big cooler out on the deck. Next, I scoop ice from his machine, spread it over the cans, and set the cooler next to Fred. He opens the lid and shoves the ice around, making sure the beer is chilled to perfection, then takes out a can, rests it on his knee, and, one-handed, cracks it open.

The Castaways board meeting begins.

The men discuss all manner of marina

business until the conversation naturally migrates to gossip. Now their attention turns to me. Of course I start with my new story, the one I just made up for Lu. But something inside me wells up and I can't stop myself from telling a yarn. I think it comes from spending too much time with old men.

"As you know, Grandmother passed and the church ladies have been taking real good care of me and talking with my aunt from Oregon." Even as I begin to speak, I remember Grandmother's warning about the lake of fire—the place liars go to when they die—and I wonder how hot it will be.

"She's getting ready to move out here and everyone has agreed I can stay on *The Karna Kathleen*. It might be the last summer I get to live on her. Of course, Aunt Linda will be spending a lot of time with me. She's really nice, but doesn't get around that well, so mostly she'll be up at the house."

By now, I'm floating outside of my body up in the sunbeams and smoke. I look down at myself and watch the words spill off my lying lips.

I go on, "*The Karna Kathleen* is in tip-top condition, but for a little mold on the carpet and siding, and I'll have that cleaned up in a day or two. I've checked and all of her systems are up and running."

Except the engines are still full of anti-freeze, and I don't know if any of the water pipes have cracked over two long winters. Oh, and I'll be living in the dark without electricity and heat. Of course, I don't tell them any of that.

From up here I watch Lu and the men shake their heads back and forth, then up and down. I'm not sure they're falling for it, but at least they aren't saying I have to leave.

Sometime later, I float back down to me, pick up my new life jacket, and get out of there as fast as I can.

I walk north up the dock, sucking in fresh air and knocking cigarette smoke off my clothes. If they come after me, it's all over. I swear I don't get any oxygen all the way back to my slip. I have no idea what I just told everyone, but I bet it's the next river rumor. Usually, the dumbest boater gets the most attention. So now, I just have to keep my head down and hope nobody notices I'm living without electricity.

I wish I had eyes in the back of my head. Grandpa always said, "You can't kid a kidder," and Pull-Apart Fred is surely watching me walk back up the dock to *The Karna Kathleen.*

Nautical Terms

vessel   a ship or large boat

tip-top condition   the highest degree of quality or excellence

river rumor   a rumor that circulates from one boater or marina to the next

7. Setting Up House

I NEED TO GET *THE KARNA KATHLEEN* READY FOR SUMMER.

Not having electricity isn't the end of the world. I have quilts, candles, and flashlights. However, I can't live without water. Back in front of my slip, I turn on the spigot. Water gushes out. Thank goodness the dock water is turned on.

In Minnesota, dock water is shut off once the weather gets cold to keep pipes from freezing. Lucky for me, Castaways' dock water is on. Winter live-aboards don't have running water down at the marina, so it's a great day when the dock water is turned back on for the summer.

After Grandpa's death we stopped heating the boat during the winter. We drained the water system so the water wouldn't freeze in the pipes and bust them. Now I need to sterilize and refill the water tank. Then I'll hook up the dock water and see if any of the pipes are cracked.

In the main cabin, I kick a pile of quilts out of the way and lift the carpeted floor hatch. I duck my head down the hole and use a flashlight to inspect the bilge. The good news is that the hull is dry. No leaks!

I'm just short enough to be able to crawl down in the bilge. Grandpa had to slide on his belly when he worked down here. Piles of red, flaky rust remind me of the surface of Mars. I hear the tap-tap-tap of hardheaded fish. They eat algae off the bottom of the hull. I had forgotten the constant noise they make in this dark underworld.

I pull our two garden hoses from stowage, climb back out of the hull, and shut the hatch. The hoses get attached to twin spigots out on the dock. One hose is for my water system and the other is for day-to-day use, like when I want to spray off the deck. That's when I realize I have another problem.

Our slip is 18 feet wide but our boat only

fills 16 feet of it. There's a two-foot gap on the starboard side between the dock and the boat. As I stand on the dock I can't reach across the gap to attach the hose to the water hook-ups on the houseboat.

In the fall, our boat was shoved to the port side of our slip. That way, we could walk down Ramp 3 and step onto our shrink-wrapped boat without having to travel the extra distance to the starboard side. It doesn't seem like that big a deal, but once the frigid weather hits, and drifts of blowing snow cover the docks, the shorter walk could be a matter of life or death, especially if one slipped into the freezing river.

Each spring, we pushed the boat back snug to the starboard side so it was easier to reach the water tank and hook-ups. That makes it quicker to unhook the utilities to take the boat out on the river. A two-foot gap doesn't sound like much. But with high water pushing the houseboat downriver to port, I need help.

The marina is quiet after a busy morning. No one is in sight. Through the trees up on the dike wall I see Scottie's Jeep parked in his spot.

73

He'll help me.

Scottie's boat is called *Wake-N-Bake*. He comes to the door with a wide smile and welcomes me in. His eyes twinkle in the afternoon sun.

"Pipps! I saw you were back! What are you doing down here?"

"I'm getting my boat ready for summer. My water tank needs filling. Can you help me shove my boat starboard?" I get right to the point. I'm not sure how much I can tell him.

"Come in. I'll grab my jacket. I hear you're selling your boat."

"No, I'm not selling it. Not this summer anyways." I enter his houseboat.

Boarding Scottie's boat is like stepping back into the 60s. His cabin has a plaid sofa and a large golden recliner. Colorful drippy candles cover a low coffee table that takes up the center of the boat. Matching end tables hold tall bronze lamps and oversized ashtrays. On the helm large agates, the size of dinosaur eggs, are cut in half and sparkle next to contorted pieces of driftwood. The floor is covered with green, shag carpet for warmth. Orange woven drapes give the small cabin a happy glow even as clouds blow in and hide the afternoon sun.

Grandpa called Scottie his guru. I loved their conversations. They would talk for hours about large cosmic ideas. While Grandpa talked about the Father, Son, and Holy Spirit, Scottie would talk about Mother Earth and the Universe as if they were alive.

"I know I heard someone say your Grandpa's boat was for sale," he insists. He pulls his sweatshirt over his tie-dyed shirt. The smell of incense follows us out of his friendly cabin.

"Nope. It's not for sale." I answer flatly.

Together we shove *The Karna Kathleen* back to her summer position. Scottie pushes her upriver while I hitch the dock lines tight to their cleats.

When we finish he looks at me with a concerned smile and asks, "Can I help you with anything else?"

"No thanks," I think of my electricity but don't mention it to Scottie. He waves as he walks back down the dock.

With *The Karna Kathleen* in her summer position, I pour a cup of bleach into the water tank and shove a hose in behind it. I turn on the faucet to fill it. Once full, the overflow valve will spill out excess bleach water. I'll let the water run for a couple of hours, flushing out the tank.

Back inside I use the flashlight to inspect the water system made of pipes strapped under the floorboards, a water tank, and the water pump. No leaks!

While the water tank is being flushed, I screw a spray nozzle on the end of the second garden hose and hose down the deck and siding all the way around the boat, cleaning most of the grime off. I wash the rag rug in a bucket of soapy water, wring it out, and hang it to dry on the south side rail.

Hours later the bleach water is flushed out of my tank and it's full of clean water, ready for use when we're out on the river.

Dock water is different. I screw the hose onto a valve that connects to pipes plumbed directly to the sinks, tub, and toilet. There's a catch. If I leave the water spigot on and the valve cracks from the pressure, the water could fill the hull, sinking the boat right in her slip. When I leave the dock I have to remember to shut off the spigot.

I screw the hose onto the valve and turn the water on full blast. The pipes are diverted around the water tank to create a closed, pressurized system. Inside I open all the faucets. Loud pops and bangs make me wonder if I've made a mistake, but the water is just pushing air out of the lines. Before long, it flows quietly.

I flush the macerator toilet. It works, running off the house battery. But the water heater is electric, so if I want hot water I'll have to boil it on the gas stove.

The boat shifts as the late-afternoon winds pick up. Temperamental clouds darken the sky and I have no choice but to stay inside. It feels gloomy with the lights off. My thoughts turn to my grandparents.

Each coped with the loss of my parents in different ways.

Grandpa found his solace on the river.

Since I was three years old, he and I were a team and sometimes we would be on the water for weeks. Life on the river absorbed our every waking hour. By the time we made it back up the hill to Grandmother's, my legs would feel like they were made of Jell-O.

After the death of my parents, Grandmother quit coming down to the river. She divided her time between home and church. While we spent summers on the river, she stayed home and grew perennials, flowers that come back every year, and vegetables she harvested and shared. Glorious flower arrangements that changed by the season were grown for funerals and special church events. She baked bars or cookies, and put together thousands of sandwiches that she reverently cut in half on the diagonal and placed on trays for gatherings in the church hall. During the long winter months, she made quilts and sewed our clothes.

In the middle of this divided sorrow, I settled. First, spending years with Grandpa on the river and then this past couple of years with Grandmother in her little house up the hill.

Today I was finally back home, but it was lonely without Grandpa rushing up and down the dock, talking to friends about boat repairs, and gossiping as only old men can.

I wasn't raised to sit doing nothing. I'm surrounded by a mess, but if I hurry I can clean it up before dark.

I start at the helm, sorting out my supplies. Moving as fast as I can, I work my way around the cabin, finding homes for each item. On the bottom of the pile I come to a blanket folded tight around rolls of five-dollar bills. I pull several bills free of their rubber band, bring the rest to the closet, and tuck the wads of cash inside winter coats. Money won't be a problem.

Now I head to the galley.

I wash off the counters and fill the cupboards in a blur. Next I scrub down the head, its first good cleaning in two years. I am on a roll. I approach the stateroom and speed up. I want this finished before dark.

I am merciless as I empty Grandpa's dresser. Drawer by drawer, I throw out his old clothing, after checking to make sure nothing is hidden in the pockets, until my fingers come to his warm wool socks. Then Grandpa's ghost reaches out to me and his big fists hug mine. I look down and his socks are wrapped around my hands. I can't throw them away. Next, I skim up against his thick flannel shirts. I force myself not to smell them. I pull a heavy plaid shirt over my jacket. It feels like Grandpa is watching me.

I push the rest of the flannels back in the drawer. Grandpa's worn river hat sits in the bottom of the last drawer and I lift it out and place it on the door hook where it belongs. Then I toss my own clothes into the dresser without bothering to fold them.

Grandpa's bedding is worn and dirty. I wrinkle my nose and get to work swapping it with soft sheets covered with tiny pink flowers and piles of warm quilts made by Grandmother. At least I'll be warm.

Night falls on Castaways Marina. Away from the prying eyes of my neighbors, I want to throw away Grandpa's old clothes and bedding along with the trash I picked up around my boat. I fill up the marina cart—shared by boaters to haul supplies—and roll it up Ramp 3. From there I head to the dumpster at the south end of the marina. A cold wind whips my hair around my face and I keep my head down as I trudge along the narrow, blacktopped road that runs along the dike wall.

Just before the tree line ends, three men approach from the south. I don't want to be seen, so I sidestep into the trees, leaving the cart parked in the shadows. The glow of a cigarette lights up the grim face of a big man. I'm sure I've seen this guy before. The hair on the back of my neck stands up. *That's it, his name is Icky.*

No one knew how Icky got his name, but rumor had it that he had been kicked out of a marina north of here and drifted south to the inner channel. Some think he's harmless, but Grandpa said we should keep our distance.

I slide deeper into the shadows. Grandpa always warned me about drifters. There are those you welcome with a hot meal and a story and those you leave alone. Icky is the kind you leave alone.

Before the men reach me they turn and walk down Ramp 1. I poke my head out to see which way they head. From Ramp 1 they can walk all the way north on the dock that runs in front of my boat. But the men don't go north. They go south. Brenda's boat is the only one this far south.

Feeling like a criminal myself, I wait until I'm sure the coast is clear. I speed the cart down to the dumpster and fling my bags into it. As I push the empty cart back past Ramp 1, I stop and listen.

Down on the dock to the south I hear Chance, Brenda's aging German shepherd, let out a possessive growl. The men clamber around on the dock. At least Brenda still has her dog.

"Brenda, hold your dog and get out here." Icky calls.

But Brenda must have let the dog go because next thing I know Chance has pushed past the men and is standing at the bottom of Ramp 1 like a sentinel. Using his large ears and long nose he inspects the windswept night for anything out of the ordinary. Like me, maybe.

"What do you want?" Brenda asks.

"Can we come in and talk?" asks Icky. "I brought a bottle. Come on, it's cold out here."

"Well, what do you want to talk about?" She seems to soften a little.

The dog huffs before heading up Ramp 1 to inspect the perimeter—and that's when I get out of there.

Once I've put the cart back in its place, I watch the moonlight reflect off the fast-moving river. I freeze when I see a large dog. At first I think it's Chance, but this dog has short black hair. He stands on shore where the forested dike wall comes down and meets the water. Slim shoulders hold a powerful head with intense eyes. His nose is up, smelling the wind. He seems smart but looks wild. Dry leaves, left over from last fall, rattle on the branches and he slips off into the windy night. I lose track of him.

Out of nowhere I think about Scottie's question. Who would tell Scottie that our boat is for sale? No one said anything to Grandmother, and Pull-Apart didn't mention it either. I'm tempted to walk down to Scottie's boat and ask him what exactly he heard. The warm glow of his drapes tells me he's still awake, but it's too late for unannounced visits.

I return to *The Karna Kathleen* and make sure the water spigot is shut off. The night feels dangerous and I wish I had dock power. I could light a candle or lantern, but my eyes have grown accustomed to the dark. Not wanting to go inside the lonely houseboat, I sink into the daybed.

I get the jitters. Call it a premonition, a knowing in my bones, but I can't shake the feeling that tonight I'm getting visitors.

Nautical Terms

stowage	space on a boat for storing items
hatch	an opening leading to a lower level, especially a hold
marina cart	see illustration (pg. 81)

8. Trespassers

THE THING ABOUT SITTING IN THE DARK ON THE RIVER IS THAT AFTER A WHILE YOU CAN SEE EVERYTHING. It's as if the water reflects every tiny bit of light and soon it's bright as day. That's why I know the men moving up the dock from Brenda's boat are the same ones I'd seen earlier. Windswept, their jackets, collars, hair, and even mustaches fly up around them as they move north in my direction.

I skirt around the daybed, step onto the starboard finger of my slip and walk to the stern of my boat. The wind has picked up on the inner channel and I hear chains rattling and waves slapping against the docks. I climb up the cold metal ladder onto the roof of the houseboat and creep above deck, staying low so I'm not silhouetted by the moon that slides in and out of clouds.

The men stop at the bottom of Ramp 3 and

I figure they'll head up the ramp and go away. Since they don't have a boat at Castaways they don't belong down here. Instead of leaving, one of them lights a cigarette, using his friends to shield the flame from the wind. Then he walks the last twenty feet to my slip.

"Look, Icky, someone moved your boat over." He points to *The Karna Kathleen.*

I peek out between the upper helm and the large stowage box to watch the man with the cigarette. He's short and wears pants held up by a rope. He talks fast and I can just barely catch his words before they fly away in the wind. He's so thin it makes me think of a string bean.

"I thought you said this boat was abandoned? . . . there's no way . . . abandoned?" He paces like he has too much energy and needs to run it off.

A second man, with long hair and a thick mustache, joins him. He pushes his hair back behind his ear, but a gust of wind jerks it back in his face. "Let's git some food, man," says Mustache. "I'm starving. Them peaches in there is good."

They've been eating my food?

Icky raises his finger to his lips to quiet String Bean and Mustache. His wide shoulders make him look powerful. He walks around to the starboard side and steps aboard my boat, his weight shifting her away from the dock.

"Knock, knock, is anybody home?" he calls.

I stay quiet, reach into the compartment under the upper helm, and feel around in the tool box. I wrap my fingers around the handle of an old hammer.

Icky yanks on the screen door and it clunks off its track. Then the unthinkable, he opens the sliding door and I hear the clapper on the brass bell rattle as his shoulder brushes past it.

Icky is in my boat!

"Anybody home then?" His yelling gets caught in his chest and he breaks into a rough cough.

I look around for help. Scottie's boat seems a million miles away, and I know Pull-Apart Fred is in bed by now.

"It's empty," Icky calls out.

String Bean and Mustache come around and join him. The boat lowers as they step onto the deck. The boat's fenders bob and creak against the dock.

"Where's all the food? Man, someone's been here." Mustache complains.

"Hey, it's all cleaned up," adds String Bean.

I hear the door shut and feel the men move around in my boat. For a long time, all I can hear are waves, leaves, and low mumblings.

What do I know about these guys? I've never seen String Bean or Mustache before. But last I heard, Icky had bought Jimi Dee's boat for a dollar after he died. But with no money for slip fees, Icky left Jimi's boat to rot on Derelict Island. I'm not letting that happen to *The Karna Kathleen*.

Finally, the three men step back onto the dock; the boat raises out of the water. The men stand below me on the starboard finger.

I look up the inner channel where the night sky meets high water. The moon comes out of the clouds and lights up my hiding place. Fear trickles down my spine. If they decide to come up top, there's no place for me to hide. I grip the hammer tighter. In the back of my mind a line comes to me, '. . . I once was lost, but now am found; was blind, but now I see.' Please don't let them see me.

"Hey, Icky, what's going on with your boat?" String Bean asks. "I mean, I've heard you talking 'bout what you're gonna do, but *really*, I can't believe . . . was here and moved all that stuff and cleared up the floor and it looks like they got the water working and cleaned up the deck . . ." String Bean fidgets and paces.

"That kid must be back," answers Icky.

"I thought the old man died? Dude, you said this boat was abandoned. What if that kid is living here?" Mustache asks.

Icky answers, "You don't have to worry. There ain't no way a little girlie can handle this boat."

"What are we gonna do?" Mustache asks Icky. "Do you suppose the engines are ready for summer?"

All three of the men walk to the end of the slip and look at the engine hatches. The moon ducks back under a cloud and I'm once again shrouded in darkness.

Icky steps onto the back of the boat and slides the back door open. He ducks his head inside and lights his cigarette, then pulls back out, closing the door again. When he stands up he's facing my direction. Maybe the flame from the cigarette ruins his night vision, or maybe Grandpa's flannel shirt is dark enough to hide me, but it feels like he's looking right at me.

"I'm not letting no girlie mess up my plans."

Mustache steps onto the back of the boat and goes to open the door, "I wonder what she did with them peaches?"

String Bean starts up, "Come on, let's git outta here. I don't want trouble. I can git me some work down here once the bigwigs come back for the summer."

"I've got some serious munchies," Mustache groans.

"Hey, knock it off. Let's git outta here. I don't want my deal messed up."

"You mean *our* deal, right?" insists Mustache.

"Yeah, sure, whatever." answers Icky. "This boat is my deal, anyways."

Loud barking gets the men's attention. It's the tall, black dog—the same one I'd seen on the dike wall earlier. He's back down by the water staring intently at the men. They see the dog too. The skinny Labrador barks at them, "I know what you're up to." Or maybe he's hungry and wants some of my food.

String Bean points, "It's that dog I told you about."

Icky waves his arms at the dog, "We don't need no stinkin' dog. BOO!" he yells.

The dog turns and runs back into the trees.

"I'm outta here," grumbles String Bean.

The trespassers look north and south, making sure no one notices them. Then they head for the ramp and cross the water to shore. Icky looks back in my direction one more time before flicking his cigarette into the river.

Once the men are gone I get mad. Still holding onto the hammer, I crawl back down the ladder and test the back sliding door. They left it cracked open so I close it tight, then creep back around to the front deck.

Their cigarette smoke lingers like a warning and I still hear Icky coughing up on the dike wall. I leave the door open to air out the boat, and enter the cabin.

It's hard to tell if they stole anything. I grab the flashlight and shine its beam around the room, keeping the light low in case they look back and see it through the trees. Grandmother's recipe box is open on the island. I close it and tuck it safely back next to the stove.

The men have broken a sacred river rule. They came aboard without the captain's permission. Unfortunately, I can't tell Fred and Lu because they'll realize how alone I am. The cold creeps into *The Karna Kathleen*. I shut the door and lock it.

One thing is clear. Things are different at Castaways.

My first night *ever* alone on my boat. I head to the stateroom and crawl into Grandpa's bed. I sit with my back against the wall. In one hand I hold the hammer. In the other I have the flashlight. I put it down to pull the quilts over me. Warped shadows and elongated light patterns bounce off the paneling and ceiling as I adjust myself under the covers.

Suddenly, a tall man appears by the state-room door. I jump and let out a scream. I roll onto my knees, tangled in quilts, and throw the hammer hard at his hat. The flashlight leaves a wide circle on the wall where the hammer hit. But there's nothing but Grandpa's old hat hanging from the back of the door. I swear I hear him cackle.

I'll never sleep again!

Now tucked back under the covers I try to stay awake, but my brain is all haywire and just shuts down.

* * *

Sometime before dawn I awake with a start. Outside a lone goose honks out in the night. Did he lose his mate? Did his mom and dad abandon him? Each spring it seems there's at least one sorry goose who has to start his whole life over again. I slip back into a lonely slumber.

9. Brenda

THE MORNING IS HALF OVER WHEN I WAKE UP. Sunlight streams through the curtains and I roll over and look out the glass door at the fast-moving river.

All around me the marina is alive with activity. On the dock neighbors work together on their projects. Birds jabber as they pillage for food. Everything is back to normal.

Was last night real? I crawl off the bed and step over the hammer on the floor.

Yes, it was.

In the head, the mirror reflects hair plastered around my worried face. I brush it and try fluffing it, but it wants to stick to my scalp. I slept in my clothes and Grandpa's flannel shirt is wrinkled. I grab my low canvas tennis shoes. Their laces had broken off into shorter and shorter pieces until finally I had to remove them all together. My shoes slip right on.

Out on the front deck I notice the screen door that Icky knocked cockeyed. I get the screwdriver and position the screen back on its track, fuming as I try to undo their trespassing.

Today my real work begins. Getting *The Karna Kathleen* river-ready is no easy feat. I could leave everything as is and just hide out, but Grandpa insisted that we keep her well maintained. Besides, the marina has a rule that each boat must be moved twice a year. This encourages owners to sell off older vessels or make expensive repairs they might not do otherwise.

Last year Castaways' board gave us a pass. I'm sure that won't happen again. This season *The Karna Kathleen* has to be driven.

I make a to-do list in my mind.

My engines are full of anti-freeze and must be opened for the season. That means I have to lift the heavy metal engine hatches without letting them slide off the back of the boat into the river. Once they're propped up, I'll need to install the batteries. We store them in the closet on trickle chargers so the extreme cold of Minnesota winters doesn't ruin them. Then I need to screw the drain plugs back in the engine blocks and open the water intake valves—they allow river water to cool the engines.

Another *must* is to pull the bubbler out from under my boat. A bubbler is an electric underwater motor with a propeller used in the winter to stir up the water so it won't freeze. Violent winter winds knock shrink-wrapped boats up against the dock, and with no bubbler to keep the waters moving, an ice-shelf develops that can cut into a boat's swinging hull like the edge of an axe.

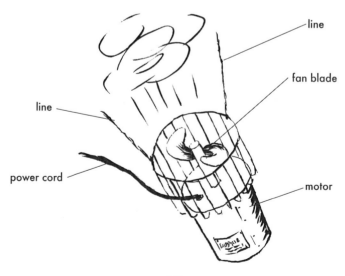

line

fan blade

line

power cord

motor

The bubblers also prevent another problem. If your boat gets frozen solid in the river, the pressure can build up and crack your hull. Keeping one side open, even just a little bit, alleviates the pressure. Some winters are so cold that we have to run the bubbler for months at a time.

I need to retrieve it, spray it off, and put it in the closet for the summer. Bubblers are expensive.

The propane line that feeds gas to the stove and heater is still hooked up to the large tank on shore for winter use. I need to convert back to the summer propane system, a smaller tank chained to the back rail of the boat.

But all that has to wait. Today I need to power wash the upper deck and siding before my summer neighbors pull in. Otherwise, I'll be blowing chunks of mold all over their boats and I'll have to clean them too.

Power washing our houseboat was always a two-man job—Grandpa and me. Alone it's much harder. I finally get the contraption— a water tank, motor, and hose—together, but then I remember I don't have electricity.

Grandpa had a 30-amp plug we hooked up to the dock when we didn't want to run power through the boat. I dig through his tools and find the big yellow attachment. It twists into the electric receptacle in the dock box. Now I plug in the extension cord. It works! I have dock power.

I start up top, aiming the powerful wand to shoot mold and mud off the large upper deck. The force of the water turns the carpeting from a dirty green to a pretty sky blue.

The previous owner used massive amounts of glue to attach outdoor carpet to the roof, and once a year Grandpa and I would take turns operating the power washer while complaining about their choice of carpet instead of fiberglass. More than once Grandpa threatened to rip it off, but ours is a vessel with no leaks and only a fool messes with that blessing.

The tedious job leaves time for my brain to wander. What is Icky scheming up? I know they were stealing food from me, but what did they want with Brenda? And most of all, what did Icky mean when he said my boat was *his* deal?

Inch by inch I shoot black and green mold everywhere. I'm not paying enough attention and just make a mess. I start over, deliberately working from fore to aft. Only halfway through the job, even my brain gets muddy. I've worried myself into such a foul mood that I decide to take a break and go check on Brenda. Not that I'm looking forward to it.

I've known Brenda since I was little. She and I were always friendly because we both love animals. She has her old German Shepard, Chance, and a cat she calls Cat.

* * *

I only went inside Brenda's boat once, back when she was at River Heights Marina. I got it in my head that Chance and Cat would like a visit, so I knocked on Brenda's boat. She pulled back a tarp that covered her door and frowned as she let me in.

Brenda's hair was tamed into a thick braid tucked down the back of her brown insulated overalls, called Carharts. In the summer she replaces her Carharts for cut-offs, revealing lean, muscular legs. Summer or winter, she wears steel-toed work boots over wool socks that fall down around her ankles.

As I entered she picked up an old rusty pistol from a box that sat near the door and tucked it into the large side pocket of her overalls.

The upper cabin reminded me of the inside of Grandpa's storage shed up at the house. Blankets were nailed right to the walls as insulation from the cold. I remember wondering, *Where does she sit?*

"It's cold in here," I had said.

"Well, come downstairs then." She pulled back another tarp and led me down narrow steps to her galley. Buckets and dishes were piled high in what looked like a mad scientist's laboratory. Brenda's water pump was broken, so she carried water to her boat in large jugs scattered around the room. In the dead of winter—when dock water is shut off—Brenda filled her water jugs from the outdoor spigot at the Holiday gas station, half a mile away.

Next to Brenda's galley was the head, a creepy looking room I wouldn't dare walk into. I joined her in the small aft cabin.

Books, army surplus blankets, and laundry were strewn across two low cots facing each other in the cluttered room. A black, insulated blanket covered the door and windows, making it feel like a cave, and the orange glow of space heaters fooled me into thinking the place was warm.

The floor was covered with scraps of carpeting and folded clothes—squashed flat and covered with thick, matted hair. Chance's tail wagged on seeing Brenda. The old watch dog didn't bother getting up from his nest. Just looking at the ancient beast made my knees creak as I squatted down to pet him. He looked the other way and his tail went still.

"Chance, be good." Brenda warned.

Cat was sleeping on the bunk and rolled on her back to stretch. I tickled her chin until she realized I wasn't Brenda and flipped onto her stomach, darting out of the room to a hiding spot up top.

Back then, Brenda and I talked mostly about the books that were piled up on the corner of her bunk. I petted Chance one more time and somehow the topic of the pistol came up. I think Brenda volunteered it.

She patted her pocket, "Don't worry about this gun. I just had to shoot it the one time. Those guys on the job site don't come any-where near me now." Brenda is in the union and operates a dirt mover on construction sites. "A lot of times I work the overnight shift. It's dark out there. Heck, I doubt that gun even works now. It's been years since I had to teach them a lesson."

Grandpa and I had agreed; I wouldn't go back in there.

* * *

Now, walking down the dock toward Bren-da's boat, I wave at Pull-Apart Fred and Davy. Fred's engine hatches are open and the men are preparing the *Credenza* for summer. The live-aboard boaters have deadlines for clearing away their winter structures and getting the marina cleaned up.

A few slips down, *Creepin Charlie*, a 60-foot Skipperliner houseboat, is being spruced up for summer. Tricia is potting plants on their front deck while Charlie carries their winter structure up to put in storage for the season. All the summer slips will fill up by Memorial Day weekend so the north end of Castaways is a hive of activity.

The other end of the dock is another story. Brenda is the only winter live-aboard on the south end of the marina. Yesterday at Pull-Apart Fred's, I heard board members say that Brenda was just barely approved to pull her boat in before winter fell on Minnesota and her tenancy had been nothing but a problem.

She leaves unfinished projects scattered on the dock and in the parking lot. Since her boat doesn't have a furnace, she used her neighbors' electrical boxes to run space heaters in her cabin. Now the board has to figure out which slip owners she stole electricity from.

As I approach Brenda's boat, I see something is terribly wrong. Her home is listing to starboard, tilted at such a sharp angle that one side of her boat sits lower than the dock. A narrow stream of water shoots out of the hull from her sub pump.

Judging by the extreme list, more river is going into the boat than coming out. The water could be pouring in through the housing in her single-screw engine, or her mushy fiberglass hull could have been crushed by ice over the long winter because she didn't own a bubbler.

Whatever the cause, one thing is clear: Brenda's boat is sinking!

Chance paces back and forth around obstacles strewn along the dock. I don't see Brenda, but I hear her swearing and banging away down in the bilge. I pet Chance who looks past me as he continues his near frantic pacing. Grandpa always said a good river dog is usually the smartest one on a boat, and Chance is worried.

From beneath the engine hatch Brenda pops her head up, greets me with her usual, "Aye, Pipps," and then ducks down to continue banging on her engine.

Cat, wild as ever, sees me and skitters up Ramp 1, disappearing into the trees.

I step aboard her boat. Some of the rails are missing and her deck is strewn with engine parts, rusted tools, and trash. Careful not to trip over the debris, I peek behind the raised engine hatch.

Brenda's bilge is rapidly filling with river water!

I don't say a word to Brenda but instead talk to the dog, "Come on, we gotta get help!"

Chance agrees. He's up Ramp 1 faster than me. We race south on the dike wall past the dumpsters, cut through the trees, and run through River Mist Marina. Down the back side of the levee is the boatyard at Twin City Marina where the mechanics are working. The barking dog gains their attention.

I follow Chance, yelling, "Brenda's boat is sinking. She needs a pump. A big one!" while Chance's barking tells them, "Hurry!"

Everyone knows the condition of Brenda's boat, and these guys understand that a sinking boat can become a much bigger problem, so they move fast.

The head mechanic rushes into the shop

and comes out with an industrial-size water pump. The two men load it onto their golf cart and take off down the gravel road that runs behind all four marinas. Chance, loyal to his mission, follows the men on the cart.

I take the shortcut, running across a vacant lot, and approach a wrecked yacht called *The Windrose*. The old wooden vessel sank years ago—not far from where Brenda's boat is sinking this very minute.

The wreck was hauled to the vacant lot and abandoned in a grove of silver maples. Saplings poke out through the rotting wood.

A familiar cough echoes from inside the boat and I slow to a halt.

Is someone hiding out in there?

Low voices mingle with the hacking. I forget about Brenda, slide along the vessel, and listen.

For a long minute all is quiet and I cup a hand to my ear, hoping to amplify any new sounds. I lean against the hull and look up while I catch my breath.

The sunshine glimmers on the silver maples

and helicopter pods spin down around me. New leaves on the branches sprout and grow right before my eyes.

Finally, my patience pays off. A muffled voice growls, "She's on my boat. But don't you worry, once them engines are opened we're going for a joy ride down the river."

String Bean asks, "Why don't ya just ask her to sell it?"

I think Icky smacks him because I hear banging around.

"I don't got *that* kind a money. Besides, that old lady died a week ago now, so that boat's practically abandoned."

Are they talking about me? No wonder they're hanging around. That's how Icky got Jimi Dee's boat after he died.

Grandpa would never let Icky have our boat. Named after my mother, our houseboat was his baby.

I want to get a look at these guys in their hideout. I creep along the weathered hull and climb up on a dead stump just below a porthole. The wood on the round window is blistered and the thick glass is covered with years of dirt. I wet a finger in my mouth, clean a small patch, and peek inside the boat.

Two angry eyes stare back at me.

Icky!

I almost fall off the stump, but I recover fast and start banging on the window. "Help! Brenda's boat is sinking. She needs help!" Then I take off running toward the marina as fast as I can.

Nautical Terms

bubbler	hung beneath or to the side of a boat and suspended by their own ropes, an underwater motor with a plastic propeller that pushes warmer water up preventing the surface of the water from freezing over. also called a de-icer
Carharts	durable outdoor apparel
aft cabin	an inside rearmost room in the vessel
list	to tilt or lean to one side because of a leak or unbalanced cargo
sub pump	a pump used to remove water that has accumulated. Also called a submersible pump
porthole	a small round window in a ship
joy ride	a fast and dangerous ride, especially one taken in a stolen vehicle

10. River Rumors

IN GRADE SCHOOL I WAS THE FASTEST KID IN MY CLASS, FASTER EVEN THAN THE BOYS. Grandmother said if I wasn't so mouthy, I wouldn't have to run so fast. I told her if I wasn't raised by such old people, the other kids wouldn't pick on me. Things only went downhill from there.

Looking back, I guess I had a chip on my shoulder. Grandpa kept the peace by hauling me off to the river, and when he died Grandmother knocked the chip all the way off. Besides, how could I be mouthy with Grandpa's ghost following me around all the time? But today, I'm not putting up with guff from anybody.

The three of them rush out and climb down a ladder leaned up against *The Windrose*. String Bean and Mustache try to catch me, but I beat them to the dock. My lungs feel like they're exploding. Icky huffs and puffs, coming in last.

At Castaways, I point to Brenda's listing

vessel, "See? I told you so."

Things have gotten worse. Brenda is still in the bilge trying to stop the leak while the mechanics prime the industrial water pump. The boat is listing so badly that tools and engine parts start roll off her deck.

Icky says, "Let's clean up this trash," before folding up into another one of his coughing fits.

String Bean and Mustache start stacking Brenda's winter structure into messy piles.

Icky looks at me and frowns, so I frown right back.

"Don't be thinking you're gonna steal *my* boat," I almost say out loud.

The big pump finally starts shooting river water back where it belongs, and it's a good thing too. There are holes in the boat's deck and if the water starts gushing into the hull the boat could end up sitting in the mud. Brenda could lose everything, then face the huge expense of raising the sunken vessel. Now the mechanics grab their tools and move Brenda out of the way to seal the leak.

Brenda comes up mad. Her pride is hurt and she can't appreciate all the money they've just saved her. To make matters worse, Brenda's hoarding ways take over. Every piece of trash on that dock is important to her.

"What the heck are you doing?" she yells at Icky, grabbing a board away from him and throwing a fit.

Old Chance has had enough and he starts barking.

"We're cleaning up your mess!" Icky yells back at her. "Hold your dog!"

I need to get out of here.

"Aunt Linda is coming to live with me," I lie, loud enough for everyone to hear. "I have to get back to my boat and finish cleaning." I hightail it up the dock, hoping my story sinks in among the chaos.

As I walk past familiar boats, I decide to share my new river rumor. Since Charlie and Tricia are out working, I start there.

"What's happening down there?" Charlie asks.

I tell them about Brenda's leak, waiting for

113

a natural opening to spread my own rumor. Finally I get the chance, "My aunt from Oregon is coming out and she'll be spending some time here in Minnesota to take care of me. Aunt Linda will be here tonight, so I have to go finish cleaning."

The more people who think I'm not alone, the better.

Tricia says, "Bring your aunt over for lunch next week, Pippi!" as Charlie runs south to see if he can help Brenda.

"She works during the week, so we'll have to plan something." My lies keep piling up.

I move on, walking north toward my slip, then stop at Jeff and Jan's boat. They're the owners of *The Windrose*, the ancient relic abandoned in the vacant lot. I wonder if they know Icky is using it for a hideout.

Jeff, a master carpenter, told me that the handsome lines on *The Windrose* are what attracted him to the wooden boat in the first place. At auction the boats were selling for top dollar. But right before the yacht came on the block, a white squall blew down in the boatyard, chasing away the other bidders. Jeff and Jan had braved the fierce storm by dashing to their car, and when the storm was over they got her for a song. She was christened *The Windrose* after the experience.

After *The Windrose* sank, they bought a boat with an aluminum hull. Jeff painted dolphins on the helm for Jan, but I never heard the name they came up with for the new boat.

Jeff is my favorite curmudgeon. I think he's cranky because he's in a lot of pain from all the woodworking he's done over the years. He slips their houseboat at Castaways at the bottom of Ramp 3 and parks backwards in the slip so people walking by will leave him alone.

But Jan is a social butterfly. When Jeff is at work her girlfriends tend to congregate on her boat where she hosts morning coffee klatches or sometimes serves up strong drinks in the afternoon. The ladies have long conversations about river life, and when Jeff comes home they all scatter. Once I tell the ladies my story, the news should travel fast.

Jan, Sally, Deb, and Barb sit out on Jan's

front deck, which faces out toward Rum Island. They invite me aboard and greet me with hugs Colorful mallards quickly tread water just beyond the boat. The sky is blue with cheerful white clouds that reflect off the fast moving river. Across the inner channel, Rum Island is in its springtime glory. Shiny new leaves cover most of the trees, and low-hanging branches meet high water.

I tell them about Aunt Linda and answer their questions as best I can, but I worry they can tell I'm lying, so I don't stick around for long.

After that, I head toward Pull-Apart Fred and Lu's boat, but the Holy Spirit admonishes me.

"Pippi, the truth protects you," it seems to scold.

The worst thing about lying is that I can't tell anyone what's really going on.

I return to my slip and try to figure out what I should do next. Well, the first thing I do is march into *The Karna Kathleen,* grab both keys out of their ignitions, and hide them in the recipe box. Unfortunately, after that, the only other thing left to do is finish power washing.

I think about what Scottie said yesterday, "I heard someone bought your boat." His certainty is what bothers me. Did Icky feed him that story or do I have even bigger problems? Scottie's Jeep is gone. I can't go ask him what he knows.

The afternoon winds pick up and the spray from the power washer blows back on my hair and clothes. By the time I finish, the sun has set. I'm cold, wet, and in a foul mood as I wrap up the extension cord and carry it into my dark, lonely boat.

I light two candles, one for the galley and the other for the head. It feels better being able to see what I'm doing.

I'm freezing. I smell like mold and need a hot bath. Using a large pot, I boil water on the stove and then balance it as I go down the steps to the head. The steaming liquid sloshes around but I hold it away so I don't get burned.

I pour the hot water into the tub and billows of fog fill the small, cold room. Drops of water sparkle on the mirror.

I add enough cold water to make my bath comfortable, strip off my soggy clothes, and roll around in an inch of lukewarm water, cleaning off the mold that's stuck to my arms and legs. My hair is so dirty that I give up being warm and wash it with shampoo under the ice-cold water from the faucet.

I dry off, and pull flannel pajamas and wool socks over my goose bumps. Then I add a sweater and another of Grandpa's flannel shirts, and wrap a towel around my wet hair so my clothes stay dry.

To get warm I heat a can of chili and eat it from the pot, standing next to the hot burner. I crush Saltine crackers into the chili and eat so fast that the crackers stick to the roof of my mouth.

I should have gone to the Holiday gas station for milk during daylight, but milk would just go sour without a refrigerator, so I mix up some cherry Kool-Aid.

After dinner I brush my teeth for the first time in days. I'll admit it feels so good that I vow to make a habit of it.

By nine o'clock I'm on the sofa wrapped in an afghan. The candle on the counter is shadow dancing. My eyelids keep shutting until a sudden weight rocks the boat. My eyes fly open.

The glow of a cigarette is the first thing I see.

Icky is back!

I peek through a crack in the heavy drapes. I recognize a glassy-eyed face and almost faint with relief. It's Brenda. I slide open the door. She just stares at me for what seems an eternity, a cigarette burning in her grease-stained fingers.

"You," she finally speaks, "You had *no* right to run for help this morning. You cost me a lot of money today. I almost had that leak fixed on my own." She points at me.

Didn't she see how much water was in her boat? Is she crazy?

"I'm so sorry. It looked like so much water. I was sure you were going to sink."

She leans closer and says, "That's what

119

everyone says, but I know better. That leak was almost sealed. Oh and by the way, do yourself a favor and turn on some lights. *Someone* might be snooping to see if your aunt is really here."

I scowl. She's talking about Icky.

Several years ago Brenda showed me an old picture of herself standing in a gym. In the picture she looked normal, with gym clothes and tennis shoes instead of work boots. Turns out she was a weightlifter, but tore some ligaments in her groin or stomach or somewhere. To this day she walks with a limp and complains about the pain.

"I'd invite you in, but Aunt Linda is asleep."

"Heck no! That's okay." She wants to be mad at me, but she can't. She shakes her head and turns to leave.

Now I feel like a heel. Brenda looks defeated. "Hey, Brenda, wait a minute. You know a lot about boats, right? We can't get my electricity to turn on. Do you have any idea why it won't work?"

She comes back to the door and nods toward her cigarette.

I point to the ashtray out on the deck.

She looks inside the darkened cabin. "Do you have a flashlight?" she asks.

Now we get down to work. Brenda goes through all the steps I had gone through earlier with the same results. No electricity. Then she shines the light on the helm. "What's this?" she points to a round black knob down on the side of the helm.

We shine the flashlight on it and read the markings. SHORE, OFF, ONAN. "Onan is the type of generator we use when we're out on the river," I chime in.

I see it dawn on Brenda's face. "This knob controls your electrical circuit so your batteries don't drain down while you're away from the dock. Someone probably shut off the power to the boat when they unplugged the bubbler." What other details have I forgotten?

She adds, "SHORE stands for *shore power.*" Then turns the large knob from OFF to SHORE. Light floods every room in my boat and shoots out the windows, reflecting off the dock, spud poles, and water. I hear a fan begin to blow in the hull, and the element on the water heater starts hissing. I'm surrounded by a soft, protective glow.

I hug Brenda, who just cringes.

"Thanks, Brenda. I better turn off the bedroom light for Aunt Linda." How quickly another lie comes.

Brenda seems happy as she leaves, and I float around the boat, closing the blinds and blowing out the candles. Then I go to bed with every light turned on.

Before I nod off I have a conversation with myself.

Is it okay that I asked Brenda for help?

Yes. Grandpa always told you, "River rats have to band together to survive on the Mississippi."

I think of all the lies spilling out of my mouth these last couple of days.

Am I really any better than Icky?

You won't be if you keep lying and sneaking around.

Was my guilty conscience talking, or was it the Holy Spirit? Maybe it was Grandpa's ghost, because it sounded exactly like something he would say.

The cold creeps into the stateroom, stealing the last bit of warmth from my nose and forehead. All at once I realize I have electricity *and* I'm still hooked up to the propane tank on shore.

I jump out of bed, dance over to the thermostat, and turn the heater *on!*

Nautical Terms

white squall   a sudden and violent windstorm with meager warning. not accompanied by black clouds. refers to white waves and broken water

11. A Rainy Day

I HAVE SO MANY DREAMS ABOUT RIVERS—AND THEN THERE'S MY REOCCURRING NIGHTMARE.

I'm at the headwaters of the Mississippi surrounded by wilderness. Old-growth pines covered by pristine white snow surround a dead pool created by a large beaver dam. A hard layer of ice grows along its edges. I float face down in the water with my eyes wide open, using a stick to write on the river bottom.

I awake in a panic and take in big gulps of air.

A cold spring rain began sometime before dawn, and projects at the marina have come to a standstill. I roll over and look out the aft glass door. The bed in Grandpa's stateroom sits below water level and makes me feel like I'm in the river's flow.

With nothing to do, I stay under the quilts and read *The Call of the Wild*.

125

Finally, hunger pangs cause me to throw back the covers and head to the galley.

Everything I packed down to the boat has to be cooked or baked. I flip through Grandmother's recipe box.

By this time, Grandpa would be driving us through McDonalds or stopping for coffee and donuts at Holiday gas station. I'm not ready to walk that far this morning.

A recipe for Peanut Butter Coconut Bars catches my attention. Do I have all of the ingredients?

Butter? Check.

Chunky peanut butter? Check.

Sugar? Check.

Vanilla? Check.

Flour, baking powder, salt? Check. Check. Check.

Sweetened coconut? Amazingly, check.

Eggs? No.

I can't bake without eggs.

I look out along the dock to see who might have eggs. The 90-foot houseboats at the north end of the marina are still empty. Their owners won't be here until it warms up. On the dike wall I make out a couple of cars.

I put on my jeans, sweatshirt, and a waterproof jacket, grab Grandpa's hat to shield my head from the rain, and walk south down the dock.

The ducks love this weather. They quack and chase each other all over the marina.

Pull-Apart Fred's truck is parked in the handicapped spot at the top of Ramp 3, but his boat is all shut up, which means he's not taking company yet. It looks like Tricia and Charlie are up, but I'm not ready to answer questions about my Aunt this morning. I keep moving south, one hand on my hat. Brenda's boat is next. She won't have eggs.

I cross the ramp to shore and take the levee all the way to Twin City Marina, two marinas down, and a good city block away. I slide down the wet, grassy bank of the levee, cut through the parking lot, and walk out onto their docks.

Captain Morgan lives on A-Dock, which runs parallel to B-, C-, D-, E-, and F-Docks. A-Dock juts so far out into the inner channel

Looking north from A-Dock at Twin City Marina toward Castaways Marina

that it leaves only enough room between the end of the docks and Rum Island for two good-sized boats to pass.

Captain Morgan has a fantastic river view from A-Dock. Looking north, she can see all of Castaways Marina. Looking south, she can see past the Old Swing Bridge and beyond, until the river finally bends west.

I step aboard Captain Morgan's boat, *Park Place*. It's a 40-foot Casa Cruiser, the Cadillac of houseboats back in the 50s. Its steel deck has a fresh coat of paint and the door is shiny with lacquer.

Maureen Morgan, known as Captain Morgan to her friends, is an energy healer who works out of her boat. She's been on the river forever. Morgan owned a restaurant in St. Paul for years and I know she'll have eggs.

I knock and Morgan calls me in. I swing the heavy door out and then step down, shutting myself into the small, beautiful cabin. I kick off my shoes and walk across soft, royal blue carpet. The handsome mahogany ceiling is arched and makes the room feel special. To my left, an ornate propane fireplace glows warm. Beyond that, on a narrow desk, sits a small computer that loops pictures of river scenes on its screen saver. If I sat here long enough, I would see pictures of Grandpa and me. Right now eagles soar across the monitor.

The other half of the room has been turned into a healing studio for Morgan's clients. A clean, white sheet covers the table she uses for energy work. When the workday is over, it folds away and the room becomes a proper salon.

When *Park Place* heads out on the river

the cabin becomes even more impressive. Its ancient engine resides under the blue carpeted, floor hatch. With the hatch raised and the curtains opened, the salon feels like a floating war room, the engine noise is deafening and all hands are on deck, especially Roger, Morgan's longtime partner who lives in St. Paul, but comes down to the river every chance he gets.

I walk across the now quiet salon and down the stairs. Morgan sits at a tidy booth tucked across from her galley. With her ear to the phone she nods a smile at me. Soft creases radiate out around calm brown eyes. With long blonde hair and a petite frame, it's hard to believe she's the same age as Grandmother.

Spread out in front of Morgan is her scheduling book and a hot cup of coffee. The steam from the coffee drifts out a cracked window. I scoot into the booth while she pencils in an appointment.

Books could be written about Captain Morgan's life. Once when we were sitting at a campfire, listening to the old men ramble on, she looked at me with knowing eyes and said,

"We women have *way* more interesting tales than any of them, but we listen to these same old stories anyway."

Evidence of Morgan's tales sit on shelves around the small booth. River rocks, shells, driftwood, and ancient-looking artifacts whisper her stories.

She puts down the phone "Pippi! Good to see you! I heard you were back on your boat. How are you?" From across the table she squeezes my hands. Captain Morgan and Jan are best friends. They must have already talked.

I update her with the rumor I made up yesterday, but move Aunt Linda's arrival back a couple of days, "My aunt will come in tomorrow. How soon before your first client gets here?"

She looks at a clock set inside a brass boat propeller, "I have time to visit if you want."

"Well, I need to get back, I'm in the middle of baking peanut butter coconut bars, but I'm out of eggs."

While Morgan goes to the miniature refrigerator, a great shriek comes from the back of the boat. O'Neal, her parrot, wants to talk. I get permission to visit the bird.

O'Neal has yellow around his eyes and lots of green feathers with a spot of blue on his forehead. I try getting him to say, "Polly wants a cracker," but he ignores me, looking out the window.

Morgan gives me a little cookie made of nuts to feed him. O'Neal holds it to his beak and eats it in small pecks while standing on one leg. When he finishes eating, he puts his foot down and looks out the window again. I guess he didn't want to talk after all.

Morgan and I walk out to the deck and she hands me two eggs. I fumble one. It splashes into the river and we watch as the current sweeps it to the end of her boat and then away under B-Dock.

"Oh no!" I wail. "I'm so sorry!"

She shakes her head and goes back inside. When she returns she holds out her hand for my egg and puts it in a baggie with the new egg. She hands me the baggie and gives me her look.

"You're being careful, right? People are talking about your boat. You're locking your doors?"

"I'm being careful," I reassure her.

Grandpa left the doors unlocked. He said we didn't have anything worth stealing, and it's expensive fixing busted doors. Besides, no one ever broke in.

But Morgan insists. "Come by anytime you want to hang out, and lock your doors!"

I give her the best smile I can muster. I'm glad she doesn't show me any sympathy because I would probably start bawling, and then I might never stop.

"Thanks again for the eggs. I'll pay you back once I get up to the store."

"Just bring me some of the peanut butter bars," she chuckles.

I handle the eggs with care, putting the baggie in my pocket.

The rain starts up again and I take a shortcut. I hop a low gate that leads to River Mist Marina's private dock. The small marina sits close to shore between A-Dock and Castaways.

I ignore the "no trespassing sign" and dash across their dock, using their ramp to get back up to the levee. It feels like I'm breaking the law and I hope Kenny Rice doesn't look out his window. The rain starts pouring, so I run.

I'm almost to Ramp 3 when I see two brown eyes staring at me out of the soggy bushes. It's the same black stray dog I saw earlier. He shakes his wet head, looking half drowned and half wild. Sleek short hair covers bony ribs.

I walk toward him. "Here, doggy. Come here, boy." But he turns and runs back into the bushes. He's cautious and won't let me near him. The rain picks up, falling heavily. I hurry back to my boat, all the while worrying about the dog.

By now I'm as hungry as that stray hound. I wolf down two pieces of toast smeared with homemade apple butter. I can't stand the silence, so I turn on the radio. Then I open the drapes and look at the recipe card.

The faded index card is written in Grandmother's careful cursive. Like all of her recipes, the original source is written in the upper, right-hand corner of the card. It says *Laverne Briggs* gave Grandmother this recipe.

Peanut Butter Coconut Bars

⅓ c. butter

½ c. peanut butter

1 c. sugar

Cream ingredients together

I add extra sugar and peanut butter.

2 eggs

I pull them from my pocket.

1 tsp. vanilla

Add to creamed mixture and stir

I crack the eggs into the bowl, then pour the vanilla into the little cap and dump it over the eggs like Grandmother used to do. On second thought I add another capful. *How can extra vanilla hurt anything?*

Add

1 c. flour

1 tsp. baking powder

¼ tsp. salt

1 c. flaked coconut (add last)

Mix thoroughly

Spread in 8 x 10 greased pan

I only have a 9 x 12 pan, so I mix in a little extra flour and coconut—something Grandmother would never have done.

Bake at 350° 25-30 minutes

I turn on the gas stove and soon a *poof* comes from inside the oven. After a few minutes, I slide the pan of peanut butter bars onto the center rack.

To pass the time I go out front and sweep rainwater from the deck into the river. The usual sadness engulfs me. The water races past and I imagine myself lying face down in the water with a stick in my hand, writing love letters to my family in the sand.

Even at the quietest times, there's always something happening on the river. A smooth piece of driftwood floats toward me, pulling me out of my reverie. I grab my pole and trap it against the dock. I get down on my knees and lift the muddy board out of the current.

It's an old, flat beam worn smooth by water and sand, and I'm curious how it might look cleaned up. I spray away the Mississippi mud with the garden hose, exposing beautiful knots and grooves in the heavy board. It will make a great shelf. I lay it across the corner rails of my front deck to dry when the sun shines again.

"Thank you, river," I say out loud, as the rain seems to peter out.

While I was down on my knees I saw extra lines tied under the dock, and remember that the bubbler needs to come out of the water. It's been in the river for two years now because our boat didn't move last summer.

I grab one of the lines that ties the bubbler in place and instantly my hands are covered with disgusting muck.

Well, keep going.

I pull and pull on the muddy line and before long here comes the bubbler up from the depths of the Mississippi. I lie flat on my stomach and hold on with my toes to leverage my weight and drag the heavy, mud-caked motor out of the water.

Suddenly, two big hands grab the bubbler and pull it out of my grasp. I look up, shocked. It's Icky! He came out of nowhere.

"Whoa! There. I got it. What are you doing

lifting a heavy thing like that all by yourself?" He stands over me holding my bubbler.

I can't speak. I get up and take my bubbler away from him. He's standing at the end of the finger between me and the dock. I feel like I'm trapped. I look behind me to the deck of *The Karna Kathleen,* my only escape route.

"Why you out here in the rain?" Now he's talking to me like I'm stupid or something.

"What are you doing here, Icky?"

"Do I have to be *doing* something?"

I change the subject. "I was just over visiting with Captain Morgan."

"Oh, how's Morgan?" He plays along.

Icky is two feet taller than me. He steps in my direction as he talks.

Just then the smell of peanut butter drifts out of *The Karna Kathleen.*

"Shoot, my food is burning. I have to go get that." I put down the bubbler and grab the garden hose that's right by my feet. I wash off my hands, spraying him a little in the process. He steps back.

"Oops, sorry." I use the space to head for

138

the boat. I turn to go inside when he finally gets to the point of his visit.

"I hear you're selling your boat. Well, I might be interested if the price is right. I knew your Grandpa. He would have wanted a man to take care of her."

"She's not for sale. I have to go now."

"We'll talk again later, girlie," he says.

I step in the boat and quietly lock the door. Over at the oven I pull out the peanut butter bars. They look perfect. I want to cut into the warm, sugary mixture right away, but they're too hot. My heart is beating from the close encounter with Icky. I act normal in case he can see inside the boat. Whatever he's up to, I can't help but feels like I've escaped something. I set the pan on half a dishtowel and cover it with the other half, just like Grandmother taught me. Then I stay in the galley until I see him leave.

After what seems like a safe amount of time, I go back out and check to make sure he's really gone. Looking up and down the dock, I don't see him, so I finish my job. I untie the second line that holds the bubbler in place, spray the bubbler and lines down, and stow everything away for the summer.

My fingers are freezing. Remembering I have hot water, I run to the sink, turn on the tap, and feel the sting of warm, luxurious water as it stabs my fingers. Then I tear into the peanut butter bars, eating an entire row and washing it down with Kool-Aid.

12. Old & New Friends

Captain Morgan has a girlfriend, Merrilee, who sometimes comes down to the river for the weekend. Once when I was having a bad day down on the island, she told me, "When you're having a rough time, ask yourself, What could be better than this?"

"'What could be better than this?' How can that help?" I asked her.

"It turns your mind around so you're thinking about better possibilities."

That's what I do now, since anything is better than thinking of Icky.

What could be better than this?

Instantly, the river answers. From the window I see two boats floating toward me from the north. One is my own dinghy, *Little Pumpkin*, driven by Steve! Hayley, his daughter, is driving their Boston Whaler. They're bringing my orange runabout to Castaways for

141

the summer.

I rush outside and Steve throws me a line for *Little Pumpkin*. I tie it off in the empty slip next to mine.

"*Little Pumpkin* is home!" I cry.

Steve is a longtime friend of Grandpa's. He stores our 14-foot runabout in his workshop across the river during the winter and knows everything there is to know about *Little Pumpkin* and *The Karna Kathleen*. I thank Steve and wave to Hayley as she slips their boat. She's a river rat too and we exchange smiles. We've spent time together on the island.

I hop down into *Little Pumpkin* to look at the work Steve has done on her.

Living on a houseboat without a little boat would be like living in a trailer without a car. Evening boat rides and island hops are impossible without a reliable dinghy. Not that *Little Pumpkin* is reliable.

Grandpa inherited her from a friend and never forgave the guy. At a glance she looks sharp. Her original owner taught auto body painting at the local community college. We

named her *Little Pumpkin* because he painted the entire boat orange, even her engine. Sure, her paint job sparkles, but the guy knew nothing about buoyancy and fiber-glassed her drain hole shut, so rain water and splashing waves don't drain properly. To make matters worse the guy covered water-soaked insulation with carpeted plywood. It never dries out. She is a slow, heavy boat.

Thankfully, Steve is a mix of mechanical genius and river rat. "I drilled the drain hole back open and added an old automatic water pump I had sitting around." His chest puffs out as he talks about the work he's done on our little boat over the winter. "Look, Pippi, there's also a battery charger. This old Johnson outboard has an undersized alternator that doesn't charge the battery fast enough. Now you can plug in an extension cord to the new trickle charger between rides to charge up your battery."

Steve is firing on all cylinders today and wants to make sure Hayley and I remember how to use a jump box.

"Listen up, girls. If your battery dies when you're out on the water, you can start up your boat using a jump box."

Steve shows us how to hook up the clamps from the jump box to the boat's battery. The red cable on the box is positive and marked with a plus sign (+). It must be clamped to the positive post on the battery, also marked with a + sign. The black cable is negative (-) and is attached to the negative post on the battery.

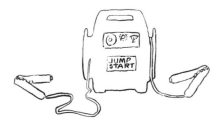

"Red to red and black to black," Steve says. "Then flip the switch on your jump box and start up your engine." He shows us how to do it, even though I've helped Grandpa do it a million times.

"But remember, you'll probably only have one charge in the jump box, so once you get the motor going you need to get back to the slip."

I stock *Little Pumpkin* with a floating seat cushion, life jackets, and a paddle. I find her fenders down in the hull and Steve helps me tie them to the cleats, so the shiny orange paint won't get chipped when the dinghy knocks up against the dock.

He points to *The Karna Kathleen.* "Are you selling?" he asks, same as everyone else.

"Nope. I'm living on it."

Steve was raised with a bunch of brothers and sisters in a house by the river in St. Paul. His father died young, leaving his mother to raise the pack of wild kids. He had a lot of freedom and doesn't think anything of me being alone at such a nice marina.

"Should we see if her engines are working then?"

"Can we?" I ask, wide-eyed.

The rain has cleared, leaving everything dripping wet, but that doesn't stop the three of us from working on *The Karna Kathleen* for the next two hours.

With the batteries attached to the engines, the drain plugs inserted in the engine blocks, and the thru-hull valves open, I return the keys to their ignitions, one key for each engine. Steve reminds me of the steps I should take to start my boat.

"First, turn on the blower." We let the blower run for five minutes. That gets rid of any gas fumes that might have built up in the engine compartment. If you don't run your blower you could have a very big explosion.

"Now let's turn over the starboard engine." I put the shifter in neutral, pump the gas throttle, and turn the key to ON. The starboard engine wheezes. "Pump the throttle again," Steve says, and it finally fires up.

We repeat the same steps on the port engine.

The throbbing engines shake the dock

while Steve inspects each motor, adjusting the engines until they idle perfectly.

There is no better feeling than being river-ready for the summer. I send my friends home with fresh peanut butter bars as a small act of appreciation, and Hayley promises to come down to the islands with her dad this summer. When Steve and Hayley are out of sight, I remove the keys from their slots at the helm and tuck them safely back in the recipe box.

As daylight fades I look out across the water to the forested dike wall, and worry over the dog living among the trees. I imagine he hunts mice and steals garbage, but he looks so skinny.

I cut up two large bars from the edge of the pan and head up Ramp 3. I whistle softly for the animal, walking north to where the marina ends in river trails and forest.

The dog sticks his head out from the under-growth. I move toward him and he turns to retreat, so I stop. Instead, I break off a piece of the bar, and toss it between the scrawny animal and myself. Then I wait.

He creeps toward the food.

I lay another piece down and back away to the ramp.

Looking first at me, and then at the food, he steps forward and devours each piece in greedy gobbles.

I toss another bite between us, stepping back a few paces.

He sniffs the air in my direction and looks at me for reassurance, coming closer with each piece of bar that I lay down. On the next to the last sweet bite we stand, almost touching, as he eats it.

I stroke his head softly and he jerks away, not used to being touched. He sniffs my fingers. I talk quietly to him, telling him I'm his friend. The rain starts again and his ears droop.

He sniffs the remaining piece of bar in my hand and his tail wags briefly.

I use the last morsel to tease him down the dock. Then the rain begins pouring and between that and the smell of peanut butter, he steps warily into the cabin. I slide the door shut, and let out a huge sigh of relief.

The wet dog shakes himself off, spraying everything with dirty water. I duck away to the galley and make two peanut butter sandwiches that I tear into bite-size pieces and lay on the floor in front of him. He gobbles the food down in great gulps, then laps up water from a bowl I find in the cupboard. More water goes on the floor than in his mouth and when he's finished he shakes himself off again.

I pull a towel out of the hall closet and dry off the skinny dog, cleaning up the puddles of water he scattered on the floor.

He is a black Labrador clearly mixed with something big. His hair is short and sleek like a Doberman's and his hind legs remind me of Scooby Doo. His feet are huge. He's still growing. His intelligent brown eyes make him seem almost human and from up close his teeth have a comical under-bite. There's no doubt he's a good dog.

The tall, handsome mutt pushes into the towel and wags his tail. Once he's dry he inspects the cabin, smelling each nook and cranny. He seems to approve of my home because he climbs onto the sofa, sitting up straight like he's in church.

Since I'm wet anyway, I go out in the rain and shut off the water spigot, then lock the door, and slide the curtains closed for the evening. The dog curls into a tight ball, but keeps a curious eye on me as I tidy up the galley and get ready for bed.

Who knows what misfortunes have befallen the poor beast. I pet him several times, hoping he'll decide to stay.

Tonight I feel a special bond with the river. It feels as if it flows through me as I drift into a grateful slumber. The river gives and the river takes away, but I'm at peace with its fickle nature.

* * *

Sometime during the night the dog climbs onto my bed and curls up behind my knees. I pull a quilt over his short hair and the river rocks us back to sleep.

Nautical Terms

water pump   a mechanical device that moves fluid
by pressure or suction

trickle charger the use of a battery regulator to regulate
charging rate and prevent overcharging

jump box   starts an engine by temporary connection
to an external portable battery device. also
called a jump starter

floating seat   a required throwable boat flotation
cushion   cushion, also great padding for hard
seats or decks on a boat

life jacket   a buoyant or inflatable vest, for sup-
porting the wearer in deep water and
preventing drowning

paddle   a pole with a broad blade at one, used
to move a small boat or canoe through
the water

fenders   a device that cushions between a boat
and a dock or between two boats to
lessen shock and prevent damage from
kinetic energy

blower   the most important ventilation source for
boats with gasoline engines, it removes
noxious fumes that may have accumulated

151

13. Prying Eyes

When I wake up the sun is shining and I swear the dog smiles at me. We jump out of bed and he explores the boat while I get dressed. He heads for the galley and lurks by the pan of bars.

I watch him lick his chops. "Just one bar for each of us," I tell him. I break a bar into pieces that he wolfs down, teeth nipping my fingers.

Suddenly his ears perk up and he runs to the door.

Knock, knock, knock.

"Whoa! Where did he come from?" Brenda asks as I slide the door open.

We join her on the front deck where Chance is waiting. The two dogs wag their tails and seem to know each other.

This morning Brenda's eyes are clear and her arms are full. "I found these and thought of you." She passes over a yellow ceramic flower pot with a drip tray attached. Sure, it's cracked down one side, but that hardly matters. Brenda hands me two more flower pots. One is green with a lattice texture and the other is a square purple pot with small chips around the rim.

I imagine them filled with flowers. "They're beautiful!" I exclaim, and place them one by one on the new driftwood shelf the river gave me the day before.

"Thought of you right away when I saw 'em."

I'm guessing she found them dumpster-diving and this is her way of apologizing for yelling at me the other night.

"My electricity is working perfectly." I remind her how she already helped me.

We follow the dogs up to the levee so they can roughhouse without knocking us into the river. They wag their tails and test each other in a game of doggy push-and-shove while I tell Brenda how I got him to come to me.

Before long he lets Brenda pet him. She holds up a giant, webbed paw. "You got yourself a great river dog." She seems knowledgeable about these things. "He's gonna be a fast swimmer."

I realize she's not looking at me. Suspicious, I brace myself, "What else is going on?"

"Pippi, I'm afraid I have to tell you something you're not gonna like."

"Is it about Icky?" I know I've made an enemy of him.

"Don't shoot the messenger, but you know Icky . . . well, he's really no good. What can I say?" She whines, as if she's the victim, not me. "Anyways, I think you need to know he snooped around your Grandmother's house and was watching your boat. He told me you're fibbing about your aunt. She's not here."

As the news sinks in, I'm surprised at how calm I remain.

I wonder who else knows.

"You should call the police and get them down here, or at least tell Pull-Apart. The way Icky is talking, your Grandpa gave him that boat. Sounds like he's planning to visit you real soon, maybe even try to take *The Karna Kathleen*."

155

Despite the sun shining and the leaves growing an inch a minute, her news makes it feel like another rainy day. I don't know what to do.

"Brenda, thanks for warning me." I shake my head.

Brenda and Chance walk back to their boat. I decide to take the black dog to the Holiday gas station, but instead he turns and trots south.

Is he running away?

I try keeping up with him, but I shouldn't have worried. The dog stops to wait for me before he's out of sight, then when he's sure I'm still following, he continues, taking the shortcut right past *The Windrose*. I stay on the gravel road, avoiding another confrontation with Icky.

The dog leads me into a neighborhood behind the marinas. We come to a small, boarded-up house on a dead-end street up against the tracks.

He sniffs and whines, wagging his tail. He goes up to a dirty front door and yelps a high-pitched bark, but no one answers. The little, tar-sided shack looks ready to be bulldozed. Every window is broken and someone dumped an old dishwasher and refrigerator at the dead end of the gravel road.

The big dog sits in a hole dug in the dirt not far from the front steps. It fits him just right and he begins whining.

So this was where he lived.

I pat his head and he gives me a sad look before wagging his tail. Then we walk around the small house looking for clues, but this time *he* follows *me*.

An old perennial garden edges the north side of the house. I recognize a bleeding heart and a thick patch of lily of the valley ready to open their tiny little bells, but the rest of the garden is crowded with fresh crab grass.

I think of Grandmother's gardens and all the years of work she put into them. Was it all for nothing?

A dilapidated garage sits behind the house. Tucked against one side is an abandoned boat full of wet leaves. Its engine is missing. The door to the garage is gone. Piled inside are old car parts and empty, dust-covered boxes.

As I turn to leave the garage I notice an empty bag of dog food torn apart. Just above the empty bag a leather leash hangs from a nail. A collar dangles from the leash. I take it off the hook and wipe off the dusty dog tag.

"Bernardo," I read out loud.

Immediately the dog wags his tail. I repeat the name, "Bernardo," and again the dog's hind end goes crazy. Then he nudges my hand so I hold the collar in front of him and he slips his head right into it. The collar hangs loosely on his neck.

"I guess you used to be bigger." I pat his bony ribs. "Well, since we're so close to the tracks let's go to Holiday and get some food."

The dog again leads the way, pulling me with his leash down a narrow path to the tracks. We walk north beside the rails to the gas station.

A local nursery has set up a makeshift greenhouse on the south end of Holiday's parking lot. Flowers, shrubs, and tomato plants line the temporary shelves. I think of my new flower pots and enter the greenhouse. The dog waits patiently while I pick out a pink geranium, a purple million-bells flower, and a lime-green asparagus fern. The lady tucks the plants in a bag and I pay her.

The smell of musty potting soil and the colorful flowers lift my spirit.

I loop the dog's leash over the water spigot on the side of the gas station and hurry in to buy dog food, milk, eggs, and a couple of chocolate donuts. When I get back outside, the dog and the leash are gone.

I look around frantically to find the dog. At the edge of the tracks I see him being led away by a large man.

Icky has my dog!

He must have seen me running on the gravel road near his hideout. Tears spring into my eyes. Bernardo looks helpless and frightened, straining on the leash held by Icky.

Icky sees me. He yanks on the leash, jerking the skinny dog's neck. Then he holds up his other hand and jingles the keys to *The Karna Kathleen*.

14. Rescue

My shriek is something awful. Like a wild banshee, I charge across the parking lot to Bernardo's rescue, with no idea what I'll do once I reach Icky. The poor animal's ears are down and he's looking for a way to escape, his back end and tail hunched in fear.

My screams yank the lady out of the makeshift greenhouse and she throws her hands up against her heart. A man pumping gas into his pickup truck stares wide-eyed, his mouth gaping open as I race across the concrete parking lot, screaming at the top of my lungs. "That man's stealing my dog!"

Icky is surprised too. He looks around, trying to act innocent while everyone stares at him.

"Bernardo, run!" I scream.

The dog spins around, pulling away from Icky, making his choice of ownership clear.

Icky spins in the opposite direction and falls back over the dog just as Bernardo slips out of his collar and races back to me.

We run to my flowers and groceries, the bag of dog food now with a tear in it. My donuts are squashed. I scoop it all into my trembling arms and, together, the dog and I run the back way down to Ramp 3.

At the boat, I'm frantic and rummage through the cabin looking to see if Icky stole anything besides my keys. Of course I didn't lock the door. I shouldn't have to lock it in broad daylight. Grandmother's recipes are in a heap on the counter next to the empty recipe box. Somehow, Icky knew right where to find them.

I run to the closet and feel in the pockets. At least he didn't steal my money, but I don't know what to do about the keys or how to get help.

My problem is all too clear. If I go to the police, they'll want to talk to an adult. They'll ship me across country. If I tell Fred and Lu, *they'll* go to the police, and sure enough, I'll have to leave the marina and go live with strangers. Either way, I lose. And if I tell no one?

The deal I made with the Holy Spirit didn't include *any* of this.

We eat—because I know how hungry the dog is—but I'm too agitated to stay still. After I eat the smashed donuts, I plant the flowers in their pots. I would like to say that the whole process is calming—as I jam the flowers in their new containers and sit them in a cheerful row on the plank the river gave me the day before—but that would be a bald-faced lie.

Instead, I plot my revenge.

15. Revenge

I STALK THE THIEVES. The gang's schedule goes like this. String Bean wakes up first and heads to work at River Heights Marina. He works all day and doesn't come back to *The Windrose* until nightfall. Icky and Mustache don't climb out of the boat until noon, and by afternoon somehow manage to drum up enough work on the docks to pay for their evening entertainment—a trip to the liquor store, then a walk down the tracks to the Holiday gas station for food and cigarettes. I follow in the shadows.

Before their schedules change, I decide to make my move.

After my stakeout, I approach the empty lot after Icky and Mustache leave for the docks. *The Windrose* doesn't belong to Icky, so I act like it's no big deal for me to climb up the wooden ladder. I have as much right to be here as he does. I just hope my keys are in there.

With Bernardo standing lookout below, I climb up the ladder to the deck of *The Windrose*.

The door is secured by a padlock. So much for searching the boat. Disappointed, I swat at some helicopter pods that have fallen from the silver maples.

"Shoot," I mutter, kicking the door with my foot.

For a second, the door bumps open. I look closer at the padlock. The back side of the latch isn't attached to anything. It's a ruse!

I open the door and step right in.

I creep down sturdy wooden steps, kicking garbage out of my way. Tree pollen and dust motes float in the sunbeams that streak into the empty yacht through portholes and short upper windows. Despite the squalor, time can't hide how beautiful *The Windrose* was in her heyday. An inlaid wooden anchor decorates the main cabin floor. Wooden panels are covered with water stains. Nests of dirty blankets and empty bottles are strewn across bunks.

I start searching. Then I hear Bernardo bark. I'm so intent on the search that the warning barely resonates.

I continue my hurried search before striking gold. Tucked in a back corner—on a rail intended for stowage of small personal items—sits Bernardo's leash. Tangled in the leash is a full pack of cigarettes and under that, the keys to *The Karna Kathleen,* sitting right there for any thief to steal.

The dog's barking changes. Someone is out there.

I pocket the keys and pick up Bernardo's leash. Then, on an impulse, grab the pack of cigarettes, tucking it into the pocket of my flannel shirt. After all, this *is* revenge.

Footsteps clomp up the ladder.

I look around for somewhere to hide. I only see one place—under a bunk. The floor is so filthy I almost say, "Forget it." Spiders and dust bunnies have made *The Windrose* their home for a long time, but I roll under the bed anyway and hope I don't see something that makes me freak out.

Huge boots come down the stairs and walk past me to the front of the boat.

Icky croons, "Girlie, I know you're in here. I seen your dog."

As quietly as possible I unroll myself from under the bunk and creep up the stairs. I almost get away when Icky yells, "Git back here, you!"

I scramble the rest of the way out of the boat, but he grabs my left ankle and I scream. I kick at him with my free leg and roll onto my back, kicking him right in the face and hitting his head with the leash. But he yanks hard, pulling me back down into the boat where I land in a heap at his feet. I don't notice that he's pulled my shoe off.

I scream, "What are you gonna do, kill me?" He releases my foot, realizing what he's done. His eyes blink rapidly and he bends down, rests his hands on his knees, and looks at me.

"I just want to talk to you. You gotta understand that you're too young to own a boat. You want me to buy it? Is that what you want? Well, I don't think I should have to, but at least let me talk to you." He breathes heavy. There's a strong smell of whisky on him. I think he's drunk.

At first I say nothing.

Then I see his fingerprints, red spots on my ankle, and I feel for damage to my backside. He doesn't look much better off than me. His coughing starts up and he favors one foot like maybe he has gout, so I play it real cool.

"We can talk," I lie.

He turns to sit down like I'm going to stay in the same room with him. Icky underestimates my speed. I sprint up the steps and practically kill myself jumping off the boat. It's a long way down, and I land in a squat and do a somersault.

The dog is waiting for me. We take off running across the vacant lot to the gravel road. We hear a bang and turn to see a shoe fly out of *The Windrose* and land with a clunk.

"Your shoe, brat!" Icky yells.

I look down at one bare foot. In my haste, I hadn't even noticed I'd lost it. Now my foot starts stinging from our mad dash on gravel.

Two years ago, I wouldn't have felt a thing—back then my callouses were thick as quarters and even these sharp pebbles didn't bother me. But my burning foot tells me I need shoes. Besides, they're the only ones that still fit me. I turn back to *The Windrose,* but Bernardo, a born retriever, is already running across the vacant lot. He picks up my shoe in his mouth, and brings it to me, wagging his tail with pride.

Inside the abandoned boat I hear a great yell come from Icky. "GIRLIE, you get back here, thief!"

The dog and I run home to *The Karna Kathleen.* The sun is out and the river is doing a happy dance, but honestly, I'm scared. I look at *Little Pumpkin* bobbing in the waves.

"Well, why not?" I ask Bernardo. "He'll never catch us out on the river. Let's let him cool off for a while."

The dog seems to be all for it.

Nautical Terms

heyday   a period of great success, popularity, or vigor

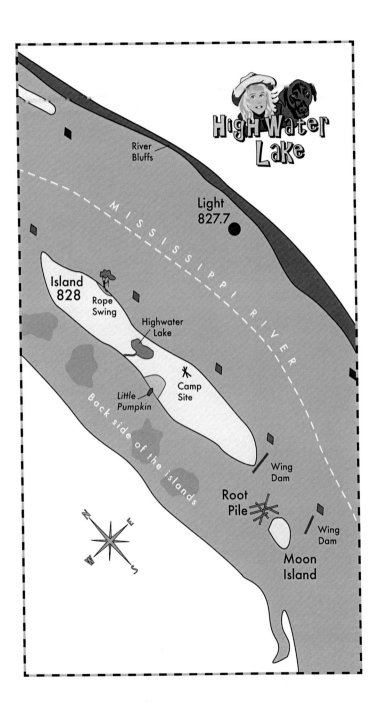

16. Back on the River

Little Pumpkin's battery is fully charged. I remove the extension cord from the trickle charger Steve mounted on its transom. It's ready to go. Most boaters don't boat this early in the season. The river is high and fast, especially with recent rains, but I don't care. I need to get away from Icky. I'm about to push off when a vague image pops into my head.

It's a dead body I saw once, or maybe there were two. I was little and Grandpa made me look the other way. A lot of people die up and down the Mississippi River each year. The memories of a gray arm floating in a pile of deadheads—and the grim look on Grandpa's face—make me jump out of *Little Pumpkin* and run back inside *The Karna Kathleen*.

In the back of the closet I find our waterproof river bag. It has everything I need to stay warm and dry out on the river, including a hatchet to chop firewood. I throw in some food for the dog and me and fill a container with water. Then I cut some bars for Morgan and wrap them in Saran Wrap.

I grab Grandpa's hat off the back hook on my way out, and lock the door. The last thing I do is put on my new life jacket and snap it closed. Now we're ready to go.

Little Pumpkin fires right up and I flip the fenders into the boat before untying it. I back out of the slip and head south. Dangerous dead-heads could be lurking just under the surface of the muddy water, but I don't care.

As I approach *Park Place,* I can tell Captain Morgan is with a client. I pull up alongside A-Dock and leave the package of peanut butter bars on her front deck. I should wait and tell her about Icky, but I don't.

We head south on the inner channel. The current is fast and in no time we are past the marinas and gas dock.

Smaller vessels avoid the main channel of the river—especially during high water. I take a short cut under the Old Swing Bridge—along the back side of Derelict Island where the last remains of Jimi Dee's boat have almost vanished. The roof of the old houseboat is all that is visible. The rest is completely submerged in the muddy Mississippi, thanks to Icky.

How did Icky end up with Jimi Dee's boat anyway? Maybe he lied about worked on it the same way he lied about working on *The Karna Kathleen*. Once Jimi Dee passed, there was no one left to claim it.

River rumor had it that someone left it tied to the island when Icky got hauled off to jail. The engines weren't winterized and the old boat didn't stand a chance. For two long years it's been polluting the river as it disintegrates.

South of Derelict Island, we merge with the main channel where the river widens to meet the sky. The day is glorious. I begin to calm down. My fear of Icky subsides.

Besides, how can you be upset surrounded by so much beauty? Nature erupts in a massive growth spurt. Along one shore a gaggle of geese teach their goslings to forage for food. The Labrador barks his hello and wags his tail.

He is a natural river dog, just like Brenda said, sitting on the front of the boat, looking around in all directions.

A family of river otters splashes on one side and I'm sure Bernardo will jump in after them, but he seems to know better. Still, he refuses to take his eyes off the otters until we are long past them. He spends the rest of the boat ride with eagle eyes scanning the shore, nose in the air, intent on finding more.

One mile, two miles, almost three miles downstream we float, swiftly passing bluffs and tree lined shores. There's not a beach in sight. High water has transformed familiar landmarks into foreign territory. Finally, the river takes a deep bend and I see the islands.

Over the years, the dredging process and the unrelenting river had eroded the land where the river turns south, creating a cluster of islands, now whittled down to just two. Ahead are 828, and just beyond it, Moon Island. Roots of long forgotten trees litter the backwaters and sit just below the surface, ready to snag a prop. The safest approach to the back side of the islands is to float past them by way of the main channel, and come back upriver behind them from the south.

I shift my engine into neutral and drift in the current past 828. The island is named for the Grey Cloud Slough Light 827.7, a channel light that sits directly across from it. River lore has it that the old timers were feeling optimistic the day they named the island 828, rounding the number up.

We drift for almost half a mile, passing the rope swing that hangs limp from the tree. Its roots and our beach have vanished under high water. Next comes Moon Island, an island that gets smaller and smaller each year. I put *Little Pumpkin* in gear and drive around its southern tip, coming back upriver on the west side of the two islands.

In the backwaters the tree branches hang down touching the water. Finally, I come to our spot, a clearing with a sandy beach that stretches up a hill to the top of 828.

Grandpa groomed this beach special for *The Karna Kathleen.* To be sure other boaters knew this was his parking spot, he nailed a big board on an old tree with a picture of a pirate's skull and a warning sign that read, *Demon's Den*. The sign was removed long ago—either by man or nature. Beaches are first-come, first-serve. That's the rule.

On the hottest days Grandpa would pull out inflated inner tubes from our hull stowage. With the boat beached firmly on the island, he would tie off inflated inner tubes to the steel rails of *The Karna Kathleen* so we could play on them in shallow backwaters without being pulled downstream.

Today I have the beach to myself.

The boat safely tied off, Bernardo and I climb up the sandy bank and head across the island to inspect the old campsite overlooking the main channel. This spot provides a rewarding view up and down the river. Across the river to the east, the afternoon sun heats up tall limestone bluffs. Breezes catch just right, and make the spot comfortable.

I spend the afternoon cleaning up our campsite. I rebuild the fire pit, digging up rocks and

Bluffs across from Island 828

setting them in a tight circle. I collect smaller driftwood along the shore and branches that have blown off trees, stacking them in a pile. By July the island will be picked clean of firewood, but for now there's plenty.

The dog has his own idea of fun.

Bernardo takes off at a gallop, exploring the island. Before long the young dog flies past me, ears and jowls flapping in the wind and a big smile on his face. He races along the river, kicking up water and sand, then runs back into the forest. When he gets thirsty he races to the river and drinks by lowering his nose under the water as he runs by. His wild instincts are on full display as he chases imaginary prey.

"Leave things better than you found them," was always our motto. Before leaving the beach, I set up a starter pile of twigs and small branches in the fire pit. Grandpa and his river friends were always impressed when a campfire was ready to go with just the strike of a match.

At suppertime the dog and I walk back to the boat and eat. He gobbles down his food and then begs for a bite of my sandwich. He gets most of it. Worn out, he hops into the boat and curls up on the carpet. I look at my river bag. I should probably just set up the tent and make camp here, but even though the day is sunny, it's going to get cold tonight.

But I'm still not sure how to handle Icky. I join the dog in *Little Pumpkin* and mull over what to do next. Icky could make another visit to *The Karna Kathleen*—especially if he's been drinking. The safest thing would be to hang out with friends. But I'm on my own.

It's a calm evening on the river. I climb in the boat and push us away from shore without starting the engine. I throw out the anchor so we won't drift south. The front bench seat is comfortable and my view of the river lulls me as we bob in the current. The colors of the sky change from gold to orange, then to a deep dark blue.

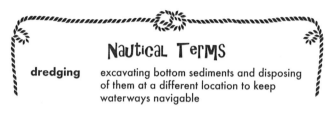

Nautical Terms

dredging   excavating bottom sediments and disposing of them at a different location to keep waterways navigable

17. Night Troubles

I dream that Icky is chasing us down the river. My eyes fly open.

I'm hanging on a hook behind 828. Night covers the Mississippi. A distant train honks at an intersection as it rumbles north toward St. Paul. A buzzing noise whirls around my head and I swat at it, thinking it's a mosquito, but it's too early in the season for bugs. It's a boat speeding downriver in my direction!

By now Pull-Apart Fred has his leg off, so I know it's not him. Captain Morgan doesn't know that I'm out on the river. No one knows. Unless . . .

Who *don't* I want it to be? That's more my luck. It's gotten colder. I put on a second jacket. The distant buzzing turns into a drone as the boat races toward the islands.

Who drives that fast in high water, especially after dark? The spring current hides dangerous deadheads and the cold river has half a mind to refreeze. I hear the boat race past on the other side of 828. It's heading south.

But then the speeding boat roars out between 828 and Moon Island. Any fool knows to make that cut with care, but this guy is clueless. He misses the wing dam—designed to keep the main channel open for tows—then races over the long, sandy foot of 828.

A pile of roots, the boneyard of a long-lost island, has collected deadheads for years just downstream of me. When the water is low it's a prominent landmark, but in high water, like now, you just have to know it's there.

Apparently unaware of the looming danger, the driver guns it. Underwater roots snag the boat's propeller. His motor stops cold.

The man clears his throat with a familiar, phlegmy hack. He chucks it over the edge of the boat. Then he bellows, "Pippi, I know you're out here."

Icky! How did he find me?

His boat is caught in the roots a thousand yards south of me. In the deep shadow of the

184

island I reach for my anchor line and pull it loose from the mud. I shake off the silt stuck to the chain and fight with a stubborn clump of clay wrapped around the anchor.

Icky's boat was going so fast it stirred up waves. The first wave rolls in across the back-water followed by another, and another, and another. Holding the muddy anchor, I have to squat to balance in the center of *Little Pumpkin*.

At first the waves are predictable, but once they hit shore, they echo back on themselves and even my sea legs can't take the chaos. I have to hold on. I give up knocking the mud off the hook and lay it in my boat. Tentacles of slime spread out on the deck.

Can this be happening? I should have stayed at the marina.

The black lab, my dog now, holds on with large webbed paws and growls before I shush him. With no anchor to hold us, we float down-stream. I paddle deeper under the cottonwoods hanging over 828. The waves ricochet back and hit us again. I use the paddle to keep from knocking into shore.

There's a channel to escape on the north end of the island, but over the years it's gotten narrower, filling in with sand. It would be hard to find in the dark. Safer to float south to the cut between 828 and Moon Island, fire up my engine, and escape north up the main river channel. To do that, I'll have to float right past Icky.

A full moon shines down on Icky and I clearly see he's in Pull-Apart Fred's boat. The jon boat is one of the most reliable on the river—if Icky hasn't busted the lower engine unit, that is. It's just like Icky to *borrow* it.

I mutter to myself, "That will teach you to leave your key in the ignition, Fred."

As a combat wounded veteran, Pull-Apart Fred believes in the honor system—leaving his jon boat available in case someone has a river emergency.

Icky wouldn't know anything about honor.

"Girlie, I know you're out here. Talk to me." Icky croons in a creepy, singsong voice. He sounds drunk.

The moonlight spreads warped shadows over his hunched shoulders. He paws at the pile of contorted roots, and from here looks like a werewolf in a flannel shirt.

"Are you gonna talk to me or not?" he bellows.

The dog growls louder and I grab his snout.

I've ridden in Fred's jon boat a million times. Everything you need for a river emergency is on Fred's boat. There's even a spare prop under the seat.

Little Pumpkin is a different story. She looks flashy, but is a slow, heavy boat. To make matters worse, *Little Pumpkin* has sat on the island all day and her ancient engine is cold. Her alternator—notorious for not charging up the battery—is another worry. I get out my jump box just in case, and hope she starts when I need her.

I feel around for the gas bulb and squeeze it. Usually, I start the engine while the anchor is still in the water, but I'm not thinking straight tonight.

Avoiding the anchor mud, I step past the

dog, pick up my paddle, and move us deeper into the trees.

"Okay, girlie." Icky takes a big breath, "I'm gonna tell you xaaactly what's going on. I did a lotta work on that houseboat and your Grandpa done give it to me. Now you give me them keys."

That liar! *The Karna Kathleen* has been sitting vacant at Castaways since Grandpa's death almost two years ago and our trusted friends have taken great care of her. Before that, Grandpa and I did all the work. Grandpa wouldn't let Icky touch her.

I put a hand on the dog's prickly back. "Shhh," I warn him.

The trees thin at the bottom of 828 and I lose my cover. I hold my breath as my boat approaches his.

He's looking south toward Moon Island. "That's it now, girlie. You talk to me! You hear?"

Does he really think I'll obey him?

Pulling on a root he falls back into the stolen boat and lands hard in his seat, then comes up looking straight at me.

Little Pumpkin floats silently through the water while the brightest moon of my life lights up my blonde hair like a beacon across the lonely river.

He's less than thirty yards away and sounds dumbfounded. "What are you doing all alone out here, girlie? Waiting for me?"

I slam the paddle down and scramble to the stern. My movements veer the boat directly toward him. I pump the bulb on the gas tank, hoping the engine will start, then jump to the wheel, slam the shifter in neutral, and turn the key. Click, click, click, nothing. The battery is dead.

A dim awareness cuts through his drunken fog. "Hey, you tryin' to get away, girlie?" He talks faster now. "Well, you can't. I got you trapped out here. Talk to me. Do you hear me? That houseboat's mine, and you're gonna give it to me. Now give me back them keys and we'll all be good."

The dog looks back and forth between Icky and me.

A wave of fear rises in me, but my stubborn streak rises up too.

Don't call me girlie!

I dive for the jump box. My fingers fumble as I hook the clamps to the dead battery. I need to make a metal-on-metal connection. Meanwhile *Little Pumpkin* bobs along in a direct beeline for Icky.

Now he jumps into action, yanking on the roots stuck in his prop. It's a race to see whose boat will start first or whether I will drift right into his arms.

"I knew your Grandpa for a long time."

My boat has drifted so close I can hear his breath rattling in his chest.

"You're just a little girlie. You can't take care of that big old houseboat all by yourself!"

I wish he'd quit saying that.

Low devilish snarls escape the dog. We're only ten feet away from him.

I jump to the helm of *Little Pumpkin,* wishing I had squeezed the primer bulb one last time. Too late, it has to start now!

I turn the key and give the engine gas. It

wheezes and coughs. I pump the throttle again and crank the key hard to the right. Finally, the motor sputters to life, coughing out black, oily exhaust.

The current drags us right to him.

He gives up on the root and lunges for my boat.

Out of the darkness the black dog snaps, barking ferociously with ears back and teeth bared.

Icky pulls away, startled by the barking dog.

I give the engine too much gas and then slam the shifter in reverse. It roars and almost jumps off its transom. Slowly we grind away, out of the reach of Icky's lying, thieving hands.

The dog unleashes hell with deep barks and snarls. Splashing through the anchor mud, he runs from front to back to front again. His hackles are up and his fangs glow in the moonlight.

"Thief!" I scream through angry tears. The boat lurches as I steer it around him with trembling hands. Every inch of me is shaking.

"I know you stole Fred's boat, and you don't

steal a US Marine's boat," I shrill. "Grandpa wouldn't even spit on the likes of you let alone give you *The Karna Kathleen*! I'll throw these keys overboard before I give them to you. *I know* where your hideout is. I'm telling everyone!" I know he can't hear me over my engine, but my tirade doesn't stop until I've navigated through the cut and we're out on the main river channel.

I take deep, gasping breaths as I turn my boat upstream against the swift current. Castaways Marina is almost three long miles away and Icky will be coming. I know *Little Pumpkin* can't outrun the jon boat. As I hit open water the wind slaps my face and I gulp in the cold night air.

Looking up the river I feel small and alone. I was only 11 years old the last time I was out on the river this late at night. I forgot how beautiful it is after dark. As I catch my breath the river transforms into a world of wonder. In all directions the sky is stunning, aglow with the moon's reflection. I begin to calm down.

Stars, planets, and fuzzy nebula fill the

firmament. The blinking lights of aircraft defy gravity, and moonlight rims the riverbanks.

Beautiful, tree-lined bluffs tower over the river's outer curve. Below them the current runs deep and dangerous. The inside curve is friendlier and in another month its shores will be full of boaters, but tonight it's just the dog and me—and Icky.

Just then, around the distant river bend closer to the Old Swing Bridge, the St. Paul Park refinery burns off gas from its smoke stacks. The red glow lights up the night and warns me, "Run! Hide!"

The onward flow of the channel barrels toward me.

Where can I hide?

Grandpa always said, "Life on the Mississippi is a series of calculated risks."

What would he do?

I think about my childhood. We kids played all over these islands. That's it! I know exactly where to hide!

Wind rushes down my jacket. I shut the middle windshield of the center console, wrap my river blanket around my shoulders, tuck my nose down in the rough fabric, and drive north.

Little Pumpkin plows through the water to the head of 828 where the current speeds up and shoots us into the narrow channel back behind the island again. I kill the engine, hoping Icky hasn't heard it. Using my paddle, I once again steer *Little Pumpkin* into the shadows of 828.

We're farther away from Icky now, a good quarter mile north of him. He's still caught up in the roots. I search for the inlet that will take me deep inside the island to the high-water lake. Usually the inlet is just a trickle on the beach, but with high water the beaches have vanished and the inlet should be a stream that I can navigate.

I float south among low hanging branches that reach down and grab at me. I duck between moonlight and shadows, praying that something will look familiar. A swirl on the surface of the water seems promising so I turn toward it, but I see in time that it's not the inlet. A lot can change on the river in two years.

Floating along the shore, I notice two large trees have fallen against one another to form a giant X. Their trunks are a natural habitat for large fishing spiders that hide in the bark down by the water and swim out to catch insects. Could these trees be hiding the narrow stream I'm looking for?

The giant X feels like it's warning me, "Do not enter."

I have no choice. I steer us between the trees, ducking low. The boat just fits under the X. I swing the paddle up in the tunnel the trees have formed, imagining great spiders with long harry legs and glowing red eyes, landing in *Little Pumpkin* to attack in the darkness. I almost shriek thinking of them, but catch myself and direct the boat along the narrow creek.

Just like that, the island takes us in.

I kneel with one leg on the front bench, leaning over the water. Overhanging branches scrape the sides of *Little Pumpkin* as I paddle along the stream. Once I have to push a log out of the way, but finally, the high-water lake opens before me.

Living on the river, we boated in all seasons, sometimes even in the winter. High-water lakes—just ponds, really—are usually only around in the spring and early summer, unless we have massive rains. This puddle has special memories.

I remembered the bucket-loads of frogs we caught in this hole. My friends, Nathan and Erich, would have let the frogs pile up for days, but each night I took the rock off the bucket, tipping them out so they could hop back to their homes in the mud. Come morning, we would start hunting them all over again.

I open the windshield and sit up front with the dog as we float in the hidden lake. His ears are cold and I rub my fingers around and around his head to keep him quiet and me calm while we wait.

Across the river Canadian geese honk out their warnings into the night. The dog moves away from me to listen.

"Quiet boy."

I hear a motor and realize Icky has freed Pull-Apart's boat from the roots. He's driving the jon boat up the channel, but instead of going back to Castaways he follows my route around the head of 828 and turns downstream behind the island. Icky knows these islands too.

His motor purrs, skips, then purrs again as he searches for me. Once I even hear, "Girlie," echo across the river and then it's quiet for a long time.

I lose track of where he is, but the dog's intelligent brown eyes shift, following sounds I can't hear. I know Icky is close.

We both jump when he revs up the motor. It sounds like he's right by the inlet to the high-water lake, but he must have given up the search. Pull-Apart's engine is not one of Icky's concerns. I hear the busted prop skipping as he speeds upriver.

From the heart of the island we hear his wake echo between islands and shore for a long time after he leaves, fooling us into thinking he's still close by.

I'm stranded—my battery is dead, and the jump box is probably out of juice. I pick up the muddy anchor and plunk it back in the water.

From my river bag I pull out the hat and mittens Grandmother had knitted for me. The life jacket will do as a pillow. I have a small tent I could set up on the island, but the boat feels safer. At least my sleeping bag will help keep me warm. I crawl into it and lie down on the front bench seat. I pull my river blanket over me to keep off the night moisture.

Up until a couple of days ago I had never slept alone. Now, I'm miles away from everyone. Strange noises stalk me in the dark. I'm glad I have Bernardo.

When Grandpa was alive and we camped on the island, I roamed free with no curfew. But sometimes, we kids would get spooked and race back to the adults. All our fears would vanish as we listened to their stories around Grandpa's glowing campfire. Soon we would be yawning and the adults would chase us off to bed.

When there were groups of families camping on the islands, *The Karna Kathleen* was always the "kids" boat. We lined up like fish on the main cabin floor, each with a pillow and sleeping bag. Before long we would be flopping around—a tangled mishmash of sandy feet, sunburned limbs, and island treasures.

The moon remembers me, I think. It leans over the trees and lights up the high-water lake with its soft glow. A lone cheeper, or maybe a spring peeper, crawls out of the mud and braves the cold to thank me for releasing his ancestors from the bucket. His rhythmic chirping calms my fears.

My lanky dog climbs on my legs and plops into a heavy ball. Soon we are tangled together as we search for warmth and space on *Little Pumpkin's* narrow bench.

I dream that Grandpa uses the moon's guiding light to tiptoe through the kid-cluttered houseboat to his own bed just down the hall.

Nautical Terms

hook   slang for anchor

sea legs   the ability to walk steadily on the deck of a boat

cut   a passage, especially so as to shorten one's route.

lower engine unit   the lower part of an engine extended down in the water including the propeller, the right angle drive gear assembly, the gear shift mechanism, the water intake port for the cooling system, and the water pump

gas bulb   see primer bulb

primer bulb   a plastic bulb that when squeezed primes the fuel line to make ready for fuel for the engine

transom   the flat surface forming the stern of a vessel

bluffs   a high steep bank or cliff

fishing spider   a large and strong hunting spider, this species is closely associated with water. Find it among aquatic vegetation at the margins of streams and rivers. It eats aquatic insects, small fish, or even small amphibians

18. Ride Sally Ride

Wisps of early morning fog hover in the pre-dawn light. It takes a moment to realize I'm not in heaven. A blue heron fishes 20 feet away. I'm warm, so I lie still and watch the notoriously shy bird walk along the boggy shore of the high-water lake. The frogs are snug and quiet in the mud. I drift back to sleep.

The morning sunshine splits through the trees when the dog wakes me. He paws at me until I sit up.

Little Pumpkin is bobbing in the secret lake near Grandpa's beach on 828 and it is a muddy mess.

I reach for my shoes that are muddy too. They remind me of my narrow escape from Icky. I tighten my jacket around me. In a brief moment of panic, I search deeper in the pocket of Grandpa's flannel shirt to make sure the keys to the houseboat are still with me. They are, and so are the cigarettes.

Bernardo hears something and he wants off the boat. I pull out the anchor and paddle us to shore. I grab my river bag and camp chair, folded up in the back hold of the boat, and throw them both overboard.

Finally, I hear what the dog heard. It's the first tow of the season. That means the bridges and locks downriver are open. Boating season has officially begun.

The dog jumps off the boat and sinks in the mud. Then he runs off. Before I climb out of the boat, I check the jump box. I hook it back up to the battery and turn the key. Click, click, click. No luck.

I follow the dog, picking my way across the muddy bank to our campsite overlooking the main river. I unfold my lawn chair in front of the campfire, glad I thought to set it up yesterday. I dig for a match in the river bag and start a fire. Then I sit in the chair wrapped in my blanket and wait for the tow.

The dog's explorations chase off the heron. It flies to the far side of the river, skimming the water with his large, ancient-looking wings. Minutes later a white egret follows him. The old heron and egret are longtime river friends. I've seen them before. Where one goes, the other soon follows.

Overhead an eagle flies in big circles searching for breakfast. From my vista on the island I look east to mile marker 827.7, sitting on its rock pile. Just past the mile marker is a line of limestone bluffs still in shadows on the east side of the river.

The morning sun makes the water look like glass, but it disguises a swift current. It's not until a fallen tree streams past that its speed is apparent.

Downriver a dozen barges are cabled to-gether and an impressive towboat pushes them upriver past a small gravel pit. It's easy to see that these barges are empty by how high they sit in the water. North of here they'll be refilled and head back downriver. The tow takes a wide turn before coming up along the bluffs. It will pass Phyllis Beach, then Moon Island, before it comes by 828.

As if drawn by a magnet, the tree floats toward the tow. Long minutes later the barges seem to swallow the tree whole. It disappears from sight and I lose track of it.

Ten minutes later the towboat passes 828. Its powerful engines churn an enormous wake that breaks up the river, sending chop and waves in all directions. River debris is knocked around on the tips of points and islands. The jarring motion of the waves chases the heron and egret to calmer waters.

Long after the tow has passed, the waves continue rebounding off the bluffs, causing the river to sparkle in the morning sun.

It's looking to be a beautiful day. For a

minute I forget that I'm stranded. With the battery and jump box both out of juice, and the pull-start on *Little Pumpkin's* old engine too difficult for me to pull, I'm lucky I packed food and water. I make myself a sandwich and eat the last of the peanut butter bars I packed in my river bag. When he smells food, Bernardo comes running.

As I sit with the dog I wonder if anyone at Castaways notices that I'm gone. I haven't talked to Fred and Lu in a couple of days and the church ladies, up on the hill, figure I'm with Aunt Linda. Captain Morgan is just waking up. None of them know where to look for me. And Icky? Would he risk his own neck and alert someone to my whereabouts? Probably not. Even now he could be jerry-rigging *The Karna Kathleen* to steal it.

As if sensing my concern, the black Labrador comes and jumps on my lap, nearly knocking the lawn chair over with his wet, muddy paws. One hind leg doesn't fit, so he stretches his toes out on the sand to hold us up like a tripod with a wagging tail.

"Bernardo," I say and he wags his tail harder. "How about we call you Barnacle Babe? What a big baby you are." He looks away, happy for the conversation.

"Bernardo," I say again, and again he wags his tail. "How did you ever get such a goofy name?" And so I continue talking nonsense with the loving beast that keeps my mind busy and my clothes caked with Mississippi mud and sand.

Even though it's early in the season, I'm not worried about being stranded for long. It's a rare sunny day when *no* boaters go down to the islands. Sooner or later someone will arrive. My major concern is what Icky will do next. In the meantime, I take his pack of cigarettes out of my pocket.

Imagine what Grandmother would say!

I smooth out my hair just thinking of her reaction. It takes a while for me to talk myself into sinning.

The old-timers on the river, most of them smokers, tap the pack on their knee before opening it, so in my clumsy way that's what I do. Then I rip off the foil, open the pack, and pull out a cigarette.

I squat down by the fire, holding the cigarette to the flame. I lean in and puff on it, making sure my hair doesn't catch fire.

At first I barely inhale. Then I walk over to the edge of the river and look for my reflection. A light wind disrupts the surface of the water. I don't think the river wants to see me smoking.

As I inhale all the way in, my lungs fill up with heat. I cough just like Icky and look around to make sure no one is watching. Bernardo covers his nose with his paw.

"Don't *you* start in on me."

Like a movie star, I hold the cigarette between my index and middle fingers and take a glamorous puff. Not so glamorously I cough until all the smoke is out of my lungs.

Next I place it between my thumb and forefinger, squint at the dog, and talk like I'm a gangster, inhaling again. After each breath in, I cough and cough until I resort to tiny puffs of smoke in and out of my mouth.

Realization dawns. I will never be a smoker.

Using my finger and thumb, I try to pinch out the coal. It burns my fingers before I finally tamp it out in the sand. Ripping off the filter, I toss it in the fire. The leftover tobacco falls out of the paper and a light breeze carries it away.

Even as the marks Icky left on my ankle turn to bruises, I rip apart each of his cigarettes, imagining it's his head I'm ripping off, until the whole pack is in the campfire.

Just then Bernardo comes to attention, pointing upriver with his head, front leg, and tail. After a spell I hear music. "The Twist" echoes off the bluffs. That can only mean one thing. Ride Sally Ride is coming down the river!

Sally is an Italian/Irish lady from St. Paul. I call her Ride Sally Ride because of the famous song "Mustang Sally." It fits because all she wants to do is ride up and down the river. The nickname is painted on the back of her pontoon.

Once the weather gets nice, Sally delivers Avon packages by boat to her friends who live on the river.

I jump up and down and wave my arms. "Saaalllyyy!" I holler across the water. Then I fan the flames on the campfire, hoping to get her attention.

Sally does a double take before turning her boat toward 828.

She scans the island as she pulls her 18-foot pontoon boat right up on the sand in front of me and I run to greet her. I hope she doesn't smell the tobacco on my fingers.

"Pippi. What on earth is going on out here?"

My fire is blazing pretty well by now and I see her glance at my lone chair.

"I got stranded here last night. My boat died. It's on the other side of the island," I explain as she looks around in disbelief.

"You poor thing. You're all alone?"

"Fortunately, I had my camping gear and food from a picnic. There were other people here last night, but after they left, my engine wouldn't start." I add, hoping to reassure her. It doesn't work. She can see I'm lying.

"Besides, I have my dog, Bernardo. He's Italian!"

Sally looks at Bernardo—all covered with sand, even on his nose—and doesn't seem impressed. After a few more questions, we agree I'll pack up my camp while she makes her delivery south and then she'll hurry back to get us.

By the time she returns I've put out the fire, paddled *Little Pumpkin* out of the high-water lake, and attached a sturdy towline to it.

Sally pulls up her pontoon and I tie off *Little Pumpkin*. She wants me to ride with her, but insists that Bernardo stay in my boat.

I direct the dog into the runabout, but it doesn't take long for his ears to droop as he realizes we will be separated. He immediately corrects the situation by hopping out of *Little Pumpkin*, running through the mud, and jumping onto Sally's pontoon.

Sally screams in fear, "I'm afraid of dogs, any dogs, especially big ones!"

"He's just a little lap dog in a big dog's body," I point out, petting Bernardo's soft ears as he gets comfortable, happy to be aboard.

She eyes Bernardo suspiciously, but soon

we are under way.

To me, Ride Sally Ride is the most glamourous person alive. She's married and calls her husband "Admirable Dave" because she thinks he is admirable. They live at Castaways on their houseboat, *Champagne Flite*, during the summer months. Champagne and fancy lamps are how I always think of her.

They also own a house, so small she calls it the Doll House, not far from the river. I was lucky to get invited to the Doll House one Christmas. I walked into her entryway and was immediately greeted by a stone angel, taller than me. Sally said it was originally used as a holy water fountain at a Catholic church. Sally had it overflowing with Christmas candy. What I remember most was her shocking pink feather Christmas tree surrounded by religious art. We drank fruit punch out of champagne glasses and I pretended it was the real thing.

Sally has a junk business called Salvage Sal's. She picks up treasures along the way in her green army truck with the floppy fenders.

When I told Grandpa I thought she was

glamorous, he had a good chuckle. He called Sally a peddler because she sells things like toe rings, fake ponytails, cigarettes, and her chewy homemade garlic pretzels—the perfect treat if you're sitting on an island wearing a toe ring. She peddles in the bars, on the islands, and up and down the river, using the money to keep their boats full of gas.

During the summer on Sundays, with Grandmother at her church up the hill, Grandpa and I would be with Admirable Dave on the front of *Champagne Flite*. We would sing gospel hymns that Dave plucked out on his mandolin while the water flowed by.

Today Sally plays "Go, Johnny, Go" and then "Shake, Rattle, and Roll," while *Little Pumpkin* bobs cheerfully behind us as we return to Castaways. My dog stares intently along the banks as he looks for river otters, but I have bigger concerns. By now Icky will be back at the marina, most likely sleeping in his hideout. But one question worries my mind.

Did Icky rat me out?

Nautical Terms

lock   an enclosed chamber in a canal, dam, etc.,
with gates at each end, for raising or lowering
vessels from one level to another by admitting
or releasing water

jerry-rigg   to fix in a crude or improvised manner

213

19. No Choice

BACK AT CASTAWAYS, SALLY PULLS INTO THE EMPTY SLIP NEXT TO *THE KARNA KATHLEEN*. Bernardo and I jump off her pontoon and I untie *Little Pumpkin's* line from her boat and hitch it securely to the dock.

I notice a police car parked on the dike wall. Pull-Apart Fred stands at the top of Ramp 3 talking with an officer.

"I wonder if they're looking for you?" Sally asks.

What does she mean by that? Does she know I'm a runaway?

"Aunt Linda doesn't know I slept on the island last night," I say, hoping that will do. Sally pays no attention to my story.

"I'll dock my pontoon and see what's going on," She says as she backs out of the neighboring slip and drives her pontoon around to the front of *Champagne Flite*.

Now I'm in a complete quandary. Do I trust my secret with river friends or should I run?

Two men walk past Fred and the policeman and come down Ramp 3 in my direction. They're not wearing uniforms so I don't think they're cops.

Nathan and Erich? Could it be? When did my river friends grow so tall?

They see me and come directly over to my boat.

"Hi, guys," I wave, relieved to see friendly faces.

"Pippi, what's going on?" they ask, motioning toward the officer.

"I have no idea. He just showed up this morning."

Nathan and Erich are brothers who spend their summers at Castaways with their mom. Erich is a year older than me, so he must be 14 years old. That makes Nathan 17.

"We really missed you last summer. You've had such tough losses." It's not long before we're all talking at once. It feels like only yesterday that we were catching frogs together. Bernardo

216

comes forward, wagging his tail. The boys rub his head and ears, getting to know him.

From the dike wall I watch Pull-Apart Fred point toward my boat. I look down the dock and wonder if Icky talked to him. If the police take me away, he'll surely try to steal *The Karna Kathleen,* even if he doesn't have the keys.

Only minutes away from being caught, it all comes down to this: adults, who don't even know me, telling me what I must do and where I must live. In that instant, I know what needs to be done.

"Do you guys have time for a boat ride? I just got the engines open and I have to take *The Karna Kathleen* out for a test run."

"Sure," says Erich, "we just have to check out Mom's slip to make sure there aren't any logs in the way. The boatyard is putting our boat in the water this afternoon."

I don't tell them to hurry. I don't tell them we'll be running from the law. "Sounds perfect. I'll get her ready to go" is all I say.

They better hurry.

I pull the keys from my pocket and go inside the boat. I put them in their slots at the helm and flip the blower on to clear any gas vapors from the engine compartment.

Important things must be readied for *The Karna Kathleen's* first ride since Grandpa's passing.

I still have to disconnect from the winter propane tank on shore and hook up to the onboard tank.

Inside the hall closet I dig through the toolbox for a large tongue and groove pliers. Back outside I turn the handle that shuts off the propane. Using the pliers, I disconnect the winter propane line and remove the expensive winter hook-up meter and regulator. Next, I attach the summer propane line to the boat regulator. I rush to the back of the boat and open the propane tank. I've never done this alone before, but I've watched Grandpa test the lines for leaks, so that's what I do next.

Using soapy water in a dish, I check for leaks at the regulator. I pour the Lemon Joy and water mixture over the connection point, and watch tiny bubbles come up. There's a propane leak. I tighten the connection. This time the soapy mixture reveals no bubbles.

With that accomplished, I hurry inside the boat and open all the blinds and curtains, giving me almost a 360° view.

I move around the boat, securing items, including the flower pots and driftwood shelf that I shove out on the dock.

It's been five minutes, but Fred is still talking with the officer.

I fire up the starboard engine and then the port, letting them warm up while Nathan and Erich take their sweet time walking back down the dock to me.

The water and the electricity need to be unhooked next.

Nathan waves to Pull-Apart Fred, who waves back at him, then he helps me disconnect the water supply hose, coiling it up near the spigot.

Back inside *The Karna Kathleen*, I switch from SHORE power to OFF and flip the inside breakers off while Erich does the same on the dock.

Over the noise of the engines I call out, "Okay, disconnect the electrical cables and let's go."

On the side of the boat Nathan carefully unscrews the big yellow 30-amp cables from *The Karna Kathleen,* leaving them laid out neatly on the dock.

"Electricity is disconnected," he hollers.

Nathan and Erich unhitch the lines on either side.

From the helm I watch a second police car arrive as Sally walks up the ramp to talk with Fred. They can hear my engines.

The Karna Kathleen fights for its freedom. *We need to go now!*

Both engines idle smoothly as the boys cast us off, Erich to port and Nathan to starboard. Just before we reach the spud poles at the end of the fingers, the brothers jump aboard.

I decide to go north. I jam both shifters into reverse and give them a little too much gas. The fast current doesn't help. It grabs our heavy aft end. We're heading backward into

Rum Island.

"Don't hit the island!" Erich yells.

I shove the port engine in gear and give it gas. That turns us starboard, and just before the 57-foot houseboat slams into Rum Island, I jam the second engine in forward and give that one gas too. Slowly, *The Karna Kathleen* pulls ahead, and we're headed up the inner channel.

Suddenly, there's an outburst of noise from the marina. Sally's shrill whistle—the whistle she makes with two fingers in her mouth when she's been drinking with the girls—is the loudest. Pull-Apart Fred hollers too, and the cops come running down Ramp 3.

But by now we're well away from the dock and they can't stop me.

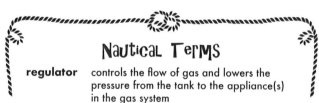

Nautical Terms

regulator	controls the flow of gas and lowers the pressure from the tank to the appliance(s) in the gas system

20. Freedom

FREEDOM—HOW SWEET YOU ARE! My boat, loose of its constraints, is free from the dock lines, cords, and cables. Me, free from prying eyes and thieving thieves. Freedom.

Ain't no anchor slowing me down. Ain't nobody telling me what to do, or where to live, or to brush my teeth and braid my hair. Ain't no one saying, "*Ain't* ain't a word and you ain't supposed to say it." Freedom.

The adrenaline has done its work and I want to shout it from the mountain top, "Don't tell no kid they can't be free because today, right now, this very minute, I am free." From the worn treads on my too tight sneakers, to the oversized hat I boosted from Grandpa, to my hair spilling out in the wind to spite it all. Freedom.

The sky is blue and the trees are covered with radiant new leaves, both to my starboard and to my port. We travel north past the head of Rum Island where a new collection of deadheads is piling up, but we fly past without any obstructions and navigate the buoys that lead us safely into the main shipping channel of the Mississippi River.

Then I start shaking.

At first it's just a quiver deep inside me. Then it trembles up my belly to the roof of my head. My hands go weak and I can't hold onto the wheel. Nathan and Erich watch my strange movements. "I can't breathe!" I want to shout, but I finally get air that comes in big gulps and I sink down, down, down into the carpet on my hands and knees and start crying my eyes out.

Nathan reaches for me and Erich takes the helm. Bernardo looks out the window, probably for river otters, and I cry and cry and cry.

I heard that if bad things happen in your childhood, it can stunt you. That's why I never wanted to be Peter Pan or Wendy. Grandpa always said to just keep being brave and I would be okay. But I don't feel brave. In fact, I'm terrified, and what a miserable time I'm having in this thing called life. And I cry and cry some more while Nathan and Erich bow their heads, and I think they almost cry too.

Wave after breath-stealing wave rolls over me as *The Karna Kathleen* heads north toward St. Paul.

This is it, the thing I've been avoiding all along, this feeling of how deep the Mississippi River really is—a deep, dark river that steals all your hope. What kind of a God would put so much grief on one girl? The full understanding of the depth of my losses comes in separate, boat-sinking waves.

Lost forever to me and the river—Grandpa.

All the hours of boating, mechanical projects, chores, campfires, old men talking shop, his soft wrinkles and eyes that twinkled, and the way he cackled and bragged when I did something amazing—gone.

I cry into Nathan's tall bony shoulder until his jacket is wet and covered with snot. Then a giant corkscrew comes and knocks me down again.

Lost forever to me and her church—Grandmother.

All the hours of cutting quilt blocks; tending the peonies, roses, and perennials; baking Christmas cookies to perfection and rolling bars in confectioner sugar; dipping homemade caramels in chocolate and paraffin wax; braiding my hair and giving hers its weekly washing each Saturday morning before wrapping her long braids back around her head; firmly holding onto reality and onto my hand—gone.

I think of the little that's left, the recipe box and the nearly empty pan of peanut butter bars, and I watch it all sink.

I catch my breath, but a great heave-ho comes and slams me back down, and this wave is the worst. Lost forever to me and the world—my mom and dad.

As the emotions crest inside me I think of all the hours of grief and loss that split my grandparents apart—Grandpa to the river, and to the church, Grandmother.

Then there's *my* anger . . .

But before the great wave breaks, Erich asks, "Should I turn it around?"

I'm brought back to the present, but unable

to speak.

He decides to make a wide turn and we head back downriver. With the water high, it's not long before we're back to Rum Island, but on the east side of the island, where the people at the marina can't see us go by. We continue southbound through the Old Swing Bridge.

I'm queerly calm. My boating experience has kicked in. I realize I haven't checked how much gas is in the tanks. Both of the gas gauges have been broken for as long as I can remember. It's better not to go too far south—the current is strong and driving back upriver could be slow going.

The early afternoon sun lights up a tiny island, just south of Derelict Island. A pile of old deadheads collecting sand and mud around its perimeter. The little beach is clear for a landing.

"There," I point, "let's pull in there."

They nod—still stunned by my outburst.

"Take the boat downstream and turn it around so we can pull up to the island against the current." I spring into action.

I run through the cabin, past the galley, down the steps, out the sliding aft door and onto the engine hatches. The propellers and waves fight each other, metal against water. I grab my shorelines, hooked to the back rail by a thick, black, bungee cord.

Nathan follows me and when he sees me attach the starboard shoreline to the aft starboard cleat, he attaches the port shoreline to the port cleat.

Then we slide between the outside rails and cabin walls—I on the starboard side and he on the port—all the way to the front of the boat. We hold our lines outside the rails, but taut so they don't spill into the water and get tangled in the props.

We meet on the front deck with two lines ready to be tossed ashore.

I go to the wheel and take over for Erich who has expertly turned the boat around. Now we are heading back upriver toward the beach. The boys prepare to jump ashore after I put the houseboat aground.

"Nate, stay on the boat and throw Erich the

starboard line first," I command. The upriver line needs to be tied off first. Without it, the current will drag us downstream.

"Then throw the port line onto the beach before you jump off the boat," I tell Nathan.

They already know what to do, but let me bark orders anyway. I think they would help me rob a bank today if I asked them. They open the front gate ready to jump ashore, as I turn the boat to port approaching the small beach—the port engine in neutral and the starboard engine still in forward. Then the port engine in forward . . .

But the boat develops a mind of its own. The red knobs of both throttles jump all the way forward. It's as if a ghost is operating them from above. Its engines roar, *The Karna Kathleen* obeys the ghost, speeds up, and slams us aground on the island. We're lucky the beach is all mud and sand, but we hit so hard our teeth rattle and everything inside the boat is jerked six inches forward, including the full-size refrigerator. The island trembles at the impact.

"I didn't do that!" I try to reassure Nathan

and Erich, who both almost flew over the rail.

We don't have time to talk. The current wants to drag us downstream.

Erich leaps off the deck. In a flash he turns to catch the starboard line from Nathan, who makes sure it doesn't snag on the rails. Erich runs north and wraps the line around a sturdy tree near the center of the small island, then he starts taking up the slack.

Nathan throws the port line overboard, jumps off the boat, and drags the line up the beach. He hitches it to a stump.

The fast current pulls the boat's tail downstream, so I gun the starboard engine, keeping her snug to shore. The current is so strong that I'm forced to crank the wheel to port as far as I can. Meanwhile, Erich and Nathan take up the slack on their lines until both lines are taut and we are firmly secured to the island. Finally, the boat safely tied to shore, I turn off the engines.

Nathan and Erich come back aboard and we hoot and holler, high-fiving each other. So much has happened in such a short time that our emotions overtake us—sorrow and celebration intertwined.

A manic freedom fills the cabin and front deck. Bernardo, sensing a party, jumps off the boat and runs to inspect the tiny island.

Then everything goes screwy.

Have you ever been sitting in a car when the car next to you starts pulling out, but you think that maybe it's your car that's moving? It's a trick your mind plays on you. Who is moving, you or them?

That is exactly how it feels on the boat. But it's not the boat that's moving. At first we aren't sure what's going on. Is it *this* island or Derelict Island that's moving? Is the shore of the river slipping off its axis? My mind whirls as the island we're beached on breaks loose.

"Get back on the boat, Bernardo!" I yell. But he ignores my command.

"Nathan, grab the dog!" Nathan jumps down and grabs the confused animal, leads him to *The Karna Kathleen,* and hoists him back on deck.

In slow motion the island slides away from

whatever had caught the floating deadheads in the first place, and at the very last minute, Erich pulls Nathan aboard.

We are adrift—the boat and the runaway island—tied together and floating down river.

Made of old tangled roots, deadheads, mud, and sand—the island pulls the houseboat around, dragging us alongside it. But it drags us sideways, and you never want your boat going sideways down a river, especially in high water. I must steer my boat, and with it, the runaway island.

I make ready to start my engines, turning on the blower and shifting each into neutral. With one hand I turn the key. With the other I pump the gas and the first engine fires up, making a strange gurgle as the propeller spins in the mud created by the moving island. I start up the second engine next, and now the propellers seem to be stirring a thick, muddy milk shake.

I put the starboard engine in gear and attempt to navigate the island to port, but the boat again has a mind of its own. The throttles pull free from my hands and are once again jammed forward, full speed ahead.

I must be going crazy. I swear the ghost is steering us again, unless . . . is someone on the roof using the upper helm?

"Erich, take the wheel!"

I run through the boat, duck out the back door, and look up top. There he is with his back to me, standing at the upper controls. It's Icky!

Nautical Terms

corkscrew	a long wave, one side breaking first as if being screwed into the ocean
heave-ho	the rise and fall of the waves or swell of the sea
aground	Resting on or touching the ground or bottom (usually involuntarily)
adrift	Afloat and unattached in any way to the shore or seabed, but not under way.

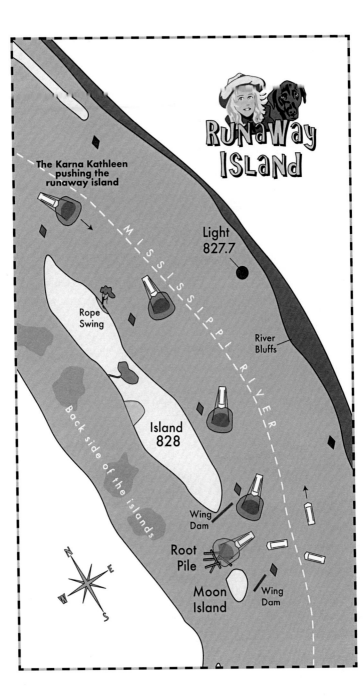

21. RuNaWay ISLaNd

Icky cranks the wheel and the island veers toward shore.

If the lines break loose, they could wrap around the props and rip out the engine shafts. We'd be rudderless—at the mercy of the unforgiving river.

I need a weapon. On the side of the boat, the steel pole with the metal point is tucked along the cabin wall. That will do. I slide it up on the deck and creep up the ladder.

I've never stabbed a walleye, let alone a grown man. *Can I stab a man? Him, I can!*

The boat is buffeted by wind and waves. I have to get him away from the helm. I charge across the upper deck!

He hears my steps, spins around, and knocks my weapon aside, but at least he's let go of the helm. Too late. The island crashes into the west bank of the river, jars the boat, and knocks us both down.

I recover first, grab the pole, and attack again.

Icky scowls and yanks it back out of my hands. Then he pulls a rusty piece of metal out of his pocket as he gets to his feet. Brenda's gun?!

"Jump off the boat or I'll shoot." He points the pistol at my chest.

I look at the frigid river, swirling around *The Karna Kathleen.* Then something dashes past my leg. A snarling demon in the form of Bernardo charges him with a vicious roar.

Icky shifts the pistol toward the leaping beast and pulls the trigger.

Fear runs down my spine, "No!"

Click, nothing.

Leaping through the air, Bernardo knocks Icky back down. His head hits the deck and his hat flies off. The gun skids overboard, bounces off the lower rail, and sinks into the river. The dog has him down and attacks his throat, canines breaking skin.

"Hold your dog! Jeez, hold your dog!" Icky

screams, rolling to fight him off.

Nathan climbs up the ladder. He doesn't know about the gun, so he scrambles to grab the snarling dog by the collar.

I grab the pole, rush forward, and push the pointed end up against Icky's neck.

"Don't ever come on my boat again," I yell. "Now *you* jump!" Jerking the point toward the water. I scream, "Nathan, let go of the dog! Now!"

Nathan releases the snarling Bernardo. He goes for Icky's throat.

Icky bellows, "Help!" scrambles to the rail, and hurls himself overboard into the river.

We watch him flail in his heavy jacket until he rips it off and swims toward Derelict Island. That's where he belongs. I bend over and pick up his greasy hat and toss it after him.

He's on his own. Besides, *The Karna Kathleen* is in trouble. The repercussions of Icky's deeds cause the runaway island to recoil off the shore. It's pushing us backward downriver.

Nathan and I leap down the ladder and pull Bernardo after us.

At the lower helm Erich fights with the throttles. "We bounced off the shore! Look at us!" His eyes are wild.

The Karna Kathleen careens starboard, its tail end spinning around like a ballerina out of control. We hit the shore again and the whole vessel tips, muddy water flows across her deck and back out her scuppers.

"Erich, move!" I step over the Captain's chair, knocked over by the impact. I slam open the side window and poke my head out to get my bearings. Wind whips into the cabin, and the throbbing of the engines echoes off the river bank.

I shift the starboard engine in reverse and the port engine in forward, gradually reversing our direction. Strapped together by the lines, *The Karna Kathleen* and the runaway island perform a giant pirouette, rotating away from yet another collision.

Now straining at her lines, the heavy runaway island drags *The Karna Kathleen* down the mighty Mississippi. Mother Nature is in command!

Inside the boat the dog paces like a predator. My knees rattle. Dragged downriver behind the runaway island, I'm not sure what to do about my engines. To be safe, I put them in neutral, ready for tangled lines, broken props, and big trouble.

It feels like my reoccurring nightmare, the part where I'm floating face down in the current, wondering which pile of deadheads the river will dump me in, abandoned by those I love to rot and fester like the bodies Grandpa found when I was little . . .

I have to snap out of it. There's no time to wallow in fear.

"Nathan, make sure all the lines are secure. Erich, check the stern." The guys spring into action, inspecting the lines, and hollering out reassurances.

"Here comes Pull-Apart Fred!" Erich yells.

My heart sinks. I'm found out. But help is on the way.

As we float along, Pull-Apart Fred and Davy speed in our direction. They keep a wide berth as they inspect our predicament.

"Can you steer it?" he yells from across the water.

"A little!"

"You have a channel marker coming up that you want to miss. Turn her to port."

I put the engines in gear and navigate the island past the green channel marker while Pull-Apart Fred and Davy keep their distance. I'm glad because I don't know what to say to them anyways.

Then we hear "Johnny B. Goode" filter through the boat. Sure enough, it's Ride Sally Ride, driving her pontoon, now in her white bedazzled cowgirl hat. Admirable Dave is with her.

Sally whistles to get my attention, "Where's Icky? We saw him on your boat!"

"Bernardo chased him overboard," I yell, barely able to speak. *They knew I was in trouble and came to help.*

Fred must have called Steve, because here he comes with Hayley in his Boston Whaler.

Then Captain Morgan and Roger pull up along the bluffs in their aluminum fishing boat.

They wear matching green river hats and Captain Morgan sends me our secret river wave. The wave means, "I'm here if you need me." She shakes her head. *Is she disappointed too?*

Jeff and Jan come alongside Roger and Morgan. Jan pulls out her video camera. Leave it to the old-timers to make a party out of this.

Unaware of my deceptions, Nathan and Erich shout back and forth with Pull-Apart Fred while the runaway island drags us south. In the middle of our flotilla, surrounded by friends, it's unlikely *The Karna Kathleen* will be ruined, so why do I feel so rotten?

Everyone else is having fun. Fred laughs at something Nathan hollers, and Hayley waves to Sally and Dave.

Out in the middle of the channel, with fast water on both sides and the sun high in the sky, an idea pops into my mind. I am the captain of *The Karna Kathleen*, at least for one more day. I yell my idea to my shipmates and Pull-Apart Fred. "Let's dump this island on the roots between 828 and Moon Island! Moon Island could use the extra mud and sand."

Fred, not afraid of taking risks either, agrees. "Sounds like a plan!"

I'll maneuver the boat so the runaway island snags on the root pile at the head of Moon Island. Then we'll have to be quick about untying the lines. It won't be easy.

Now everyone jumps into action. Admirable Dave and Ride Sally Ride circle back behind my boat and pull up next to Roger and Morgan. Steve and Hayley race ahead to scope out 828 and Moon Island, and Fred and Davy drive around the runaway island, then return to my side.

It doesn't take long for the island to pull us downriver. I steer the boat to stay in the channel as the river takes a turn. We approach 828 when Steve and Hayley come speeding back. Steve talks to Fred and then Fred drives over to my window.

"Pippi," he yells over the noise of the engines, "You have to guide the island across the foot of 828. If it starts breaking up, cut the lines and get out of there. You only have one shot at it."

I give both engines small revs of gas to be sure they'll respond when I put them in gear. Island 828 and Moon Island will be along my starboard side. I need to get in position so the runaway island doesn't drag us downriver past our target.

I'm counting on the same roots that had snagged Icky the night before to save me once again. The goal is to land the floating island on the submerged deadheads in the cut.

We come to 828. I put my starboard engine in reverse. There is no visible response. Then I put the port engine in forward, trying to turn the runaway island.

"Give 'em gas! Give your engines gas!" both Fred and Steve yell.

I grit my teeth and gun both engines. Ever so slowly a shift begins. The island starts spinning to starboard, taking its own sweet time. We are halfway past 828 and still not in position. I jam the starboard engine in forward and turn the wheel all the way right. The island shifts closer to 828, but with both engines in gear, we speed up.

Today Mother Nature is with me. Just in time, we hit the mark and *The Karna Kathleen* pushes the runaway island across the foot of 828. But I come in at an angle and my starboard prop hits sand. The starboard engine stalls.

The longest minute of my life ticks past as I let the boat drift south to deeper water. I turn the key and the engine fires back up. Relieved, I pilot the runaway island through the cut and we come to the root pile.

The boys wait at the stern of *The Karna Kathleen.* The plan is for them to each cut the lines at the aft cleats when Pull-Apart Fred gives the signal.

"Cut the lines. Now!" Fred yells.

There is too much pressure to just untie the lines, so Nathan and Erich saw on them with sharp knives. They work together, timing it just right, and both 100-foot lines float free of *The Karna Kathleen* and follow along after the island to clump up on the sand.

The runaway island drifts for a few seconds, a floating beach. Then the root pile reaches up and snags the runaway island like it has snagged so many before.

"Put your boat in reverse, Pippi." Fred yells, "Git outta there!"

The Karna Kathleen slowly responds, backing away from peril. It's a miracle that I don't hit Moon Island or the wing dam that lurks somewhere below the surface. We back out and return to the safety of the channel.

Fred and Davy are always open for some action of their own. Fred drives the front of the jon boat up onto the Runaway Island and Davy wades out to collect the lines. Once Davy has them back in the jon boat, he begins coiling them while Fred drives over to meet us.

"Pippi, let's get your boat back to Castaways," Fred directs, "We'll do a bonfire at the marina fire pit."

He makes it sound like everything is going to be okay. But I know otherwise. The adrenaline flows out of my body, my sweat dries, and I feel cold.

All my river friends have found me out. For sure, I'll be shipped across country to live with Aunt Linda, or worse, I'll be a "ward of the state."

I can't help but think of the sad, lonely waves that knocked me down earlier.

I have half a mind to turn the boat south and run, but it wouldn't be right. I get quiet, nod at Fred, and turn the boat toward home. But I go real slow. I figure this will be the last time I ever pilot *The Karna Kathleen*.

We leave the fate of the runaway island to Mother Nature. Someday it will disappear, hiding just under the water to become a trap for unsuspecting boaters who don't know the history of this place. Experienced boaters know to talk to the locals about hazards. They know that the inside curve of a river tends to be shallow, and to watch for sand at the foot of an island.

But whether you're a veteran or a virgin river runner, no one knows what adventure waits just around the next bend of the Mississippi River.

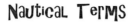

Nautical Terms

propeller — a type of fan that transmits power by converting rotational motion into thrust

prop — short for propeller

engine shaft — the mechanism between the engine and the propeller that turns the propeller (other parts not listed)

rudderless — unable to control a boats direction with the rudder

scuppers — a hole in a boat's deck that allows water to drain overboard

bearing — comprehension of one's position relative to their location

navigate — plan and direct the route or course of a ship

wing dam — a manmade underwater barrier that forces water into a fast-moving center channel, keeping sediment from accumulating

22. River Family

As *The Karna Kathleen* chugs upriver to Castaways, I wonder how much fuel she has in her tanks. Nathan takes the helm, and I climb out the back door. The yardstick is tucked under the siding, right where Grandpa left it.

I unscrew the port gas cap and push the yardstick down, tapping it on the bottom of the tank before pulling it back out. The port tank has six inches of gas.

Once the gas from the first tank evaporates off the stick, I repeat the procedure on the second tank. That tank was installed more recently and is narrower. The starboard tank has ten inches of fuel. Gas will not be a problem.

River captains know the importance of inspecting their vessel underway. I lean over the back rail and make sure water spurts out of her flappers. If water isn't flowing through an engine, it will overheat. The engines rumble like a pack of Harley Davidsons. They are working just fine.

The riverbanks are in bloom. Wild river irises reign supreme in purple turned-up capes that glow in the sun. Bees buzz around the pollen-filled pistons of wild columbines. Flowering river weeds are already knee-high.

In my fantasy, the wildlife living along the river come out to say goodbye. Fish and river otters splash while turtles sun themselves on logs. Deer wiggle their ears and coyotes lift their noses. Eagles, wood ducks, and endangered osprey call out sad cries of farewell.

Looking downriver, I dream of a day when all 2,000 miles of the Mississippi River might be this pristine, all the way to New Orleans.

To the east I see Jeff and Jan's pontoon with Captain Morgan and Roger aboard—their aluminum boat in tow. The girls are having a good old time. Captain Morgan and Jan stand in the pontoon, shadow-dancing against the golden bluffs as the glow of the setting sun does its magic.

The last time I docked *The Karna Kathleen,*

Grandpa died. I never felt guilty about that. This is where he would have wanted to be.

I stand with my hands on my hips, striking another of his poses to muster up courage. My final test will be landing the boat in her slip during high water. I take off his hat and wave at Jeff's pontoon. Shadows on the bluff wave back.

After one more long look around, I duck inside the boat, shutting out the noise of the engines.

Lamp shades jiggle, curtains blow, and dishes rattle with the boat underway. The front sliding door is wide open. While Nathan pilots the boat, Erich and Bernardo stand watch out on the deck, looking for deadheads.

With my hair blowing around my head, I watch from the open doorway. I give Nathan and Erich an update.

"No worries," I assure them, "We have plenty of gas."

Sooner than I would like, we come to Derelict Island. I take the helm. There's no sign of Icky on the island. He must have been picked up already.

We pass through the Old Swing Bridge, where I must zig to port and then zag to starboard to enter the south end of the inner channel.

Navigating the boat, my 90-degree zig to port is perfect. We're in the tight channel that runs parallel with the bridge. I lower my throttle as we enter the no-wake zone. The current is strong. It pushes the boat downriver toward the bridge's rock piers. I speed back up for optimum control. My heart starts pounding in my chest.

The 90-degree zag is another story. I'm going fast and make the turn late. We're too close to the gas dock. We all hold our breath as the tail end of the 57-foot vessel just skims past it.

It feels like we are sidewinding, the stern swinging closer to the docks than the bow. I'm terrified that our port side will hit every dock along River Heights Marina. My heart bangs against my ribs and my head gets hot.

Twin City Marina comes next. *Lyle's Style* is moored at the end of B-Dock. The stern of our boat taps one of his fenders. It's not the first time Lyle's been sideswiped.

Finally, the inner channel widens. We pass River Mist Marina, tucked safely out of the way, and approach Castaways.

Fred must have radioed ahead because Scottie is already at the marina fire pit. The bonfire is smoking, ready to ignite. My mouth goes dry as I prepare to dock us.

I slow way down to make sure I find the correct slip. Castaways' row of 42 slips all look about the same. Captains have been known to pull into their neighbor's slip and then they have to cast off and do it all over again. I shouldn't have worried because Davy stands at the end of my port finger, and Steve stands on the starboard side.

Erich is on the deck ready with the line. He'll throw it to Davy once we're close enough.

I turn the boat to port, port engine in reverse and starboard engine in forward, to get us into position. Once Davy hitches the line, I'll use the spud pole as a fulcrum and pivot the boat into her slip. I pull in upriver, letting *The*

Karna Kathleen drift home. With only a few feet to go, I make careful adjustments . . .

"Nice and easy," Davy and Steve yell.

Someone is always yelling during this delicate operation.

"Perfect!" Fred jinxes me.

I panic and hit the throttles instead of the shifters and the boat jerks wildly.

"Throw the line," I yell.

Davy catches the line, but the front end of the boat misses the spud pole and drifts south, so Davy has to release it. Erich drags the line back on board.

We circle the boat around, ready to try it again. Soon well-meaning boaters are yelling advice while I do the dance of this engine, then that engine, then this, then that, and it sounds like people are having heart attacks or maybe epiphanies. The shouting goes on until, *praise be to the Father*, I finally wrangle the boat into her slip.

I turn off the engines and walk over to the panting dog, reassuring him as he nuzzles my hand.

"It's okay, Bernardo, we're home." But my words sound hollow. This *was* home, but now what? *Will they let me keep my dog?*

I supervise tying off my boat and reconnect the electricity and water while there's still enough light. Nathan, Erich, and I agree to meet at the fire pit.

Sooner than I'd like, it's just Pull-Apart Fred and me. He stands on the deck, leaning against the daybed. "Well it was the darnedest thing this morning. I come outside and my jon boat had been moved. I asked around to see who might have moved it. I'll admit, I thought it might have been you. But when I took a closer look I realized the prop was bent to high heaven. That's not something you would keep to yourself." Fred looks me square in the eyes. "I asked around and no one had seen you, so I started worrying. I called the police to investigate, and here you came with Sally. Well, seeing *Little Pumpkin* in tow, that answered the question about you, but there was still the question of the bent prop."

Bernardo hops up on the daybed, resting

his head on the back of it so Fred can scratch his ears while he talks.

"Anyways," Fred continues, "When you fired up your engines, I thought maybe you were just getting them ready for summer. Then you pulled out of your slip and I almost fell off the dock." Fred waves his arms to demonstrate his alarm.

"When you pulled upriver, there Icky was, hiding in plain sight on your upper deck. We put two and two together and realized he was hiding from the police and figured you were in trouble. We took to the river, following your course north, but it took a while to realize you had turned back south, or we would have been there sooner."

I hang my head. It's hard looking at him. "I thought you called the cops to take me away. Icky's been on a rampage. He stole the keys to *The Karna Kathleen* and . . . well, it's a long story, but I thought I had to run away."

Fred confesses, "Since we're putting all our cards on the table, I'll admit that I did call someone about you, but not the cops. I had your Grandpa's emergency contacts in his marina paperwork. I called your Aunt Linda a couple of days ago. Your Aunt Linda will be here tonight. Good thing we got you back in one piece. Promise me you'll be at the bonfire?"

"I'll be there," I promise.

I take Bernardo up to land so he can relieve himself. I could still run away, but I don't. Anyways, there's no way I'm leaving *The Karna Kathleen* until I know she's safe.

I feed the animal his supper, take a quick bath, then set the flower pots back on the driftwood shelf before we walk down the dock to the fire pit. The campsite sits in a grassy patch alongside Ramp 2 where the levee evens out before it slopes down to the water.

The mood is festive as I approach the bonfire. About 15 boaters have arrived. They part when I enter because tonight I am the star since the river event happened to me. But I don't feel like a star. I feel alone in the crowd.

Bernardo thinks the fanfare is for him. Enjoying the limelight, he greets each person, sniffing and wagging. Soon enough, things quiet down.

Boaters share dishes at our campfire. I bring a two-quart jar of canned peaches. Nathan and Erich's mom brings hot dogs that we roast on fresh twigs we cut from the bushes. We are hungry and balance thin paper plates piled high with food, and find a quiet spot to compare our adventure among ourselves.

Erich starts, "I had no idea what was going on with you guys up top. I only knew the throttles had a mind of their own."

Before long, it seems everyone is gathered around listening to each of our versions of what had happened with Icky and the runaway island.

"Icky had a gun?" Pull-Apart asks.

"I think it might have been Brenda's," I say. "She told me it was rusty and hadn't been used in a long time. It's at the bottom of the river now. What will happen to Icky?"

"The police sent a launch to pick him up from the island, but he wasn't there. Someone else must have rescued him. He's out there somewhere," Fred says. "I hope we've seen the last of him."

Ride Sally Ride arrives late and quiets us down with her loud whistle. She's with a strange woman who looks oddly familiar.

The fire crackles and pops.

"Pippi," Sally says loud enough for the group to hear, "I just learned that you have never met your aunt before! Well, here she is. Everyone say *hi* to Pippi's Aunt Linda." Murmurs of welcome are heard around the fire pit.

I look closely at the woman. She's tall like my father and has his soft hazel eyes I remember from photographs. She leans down and wraps her arms around me, hugging me tight.

She eyes me carefully and then gives me a smile. "I'm so sorry you had to go through this alone," she says. "You and I are the only family we have left now."

I look around at my river family, and know that's not completely true.

"I hope you won't mind if I move into your Grandmother's house and work from there this summer. That will leave us time on evenings and weekends to get to know each other, and maybe you can teach me how to houseboat."

Fred chimes in, "You've done a good job, kid. I told your aunt that we've agreed to keep an eye on you while you stay on your boat—if you can stay out of trouble that is." His voice sounds skeptical.

Inside I feel myself start to shake, and the next thing I know I'm crying like a baby, but this time the tears aren't just sad.

As if he knows what's going on, Bernardo starts running around like a crazy dog. I point him out to Aunt Linda, and then walk around the campsite, introducing my friends to her.

I watch Aunt Linda's reactions to each of them, and her kind eyes watch me back. When I start yawning she pulls me aside and says, "It's been a long day for both of us. I'd love to see your houseboat."

We say goodnight to the group and walk down the dock with Bernardo following close behind.

Halfway to my boat she stops and takes in the night. She seems in awe when she says,

"The river is so beautiful after dark."

The moon likes Aunt Linda, I think. It nods her a welcome that reflects down the inner channel. The sparks from the fire explode in celebration and shimmer off the trees that surround the fire pit. On the far side of the Mississippi, downriver from the Old Swing Bridge, the St. Paul Park Refinery shoots blood red flames into the southern sky.

Aunt Linda reaches for my hands and covers them with hers, "Oh, this is exciting!" she exclaims.

I smile and say to myself, *I hope she never lets go.*

Nautical Terms

pilot   a mariner who maneuvers a ship
fulcrum   the support about which to pivot

Acknowledgments

I am extremely grateful to Jerri Farris for her editorial direction and guidance, piloting *Pippi on the Mississippi* to the next level. Jerri was also the first person to call me an author. Her inspiration will always be remembered. When Dan Kellams first walked in the room, I knew we would work together. The editorial genius and expertise of Dan are gifts from above. I especially thank Holly Chapman for her sharp edits and proof-reading. I am fortunate for such talented people in my life. Thanks to technical editors Ken Gauw and Thomas Royston for their boating and river knowledge. Thanks to Fred Bell, Sally Pilla-Perry, Sandy Buckley, and Dawn Brodey for reading drafts of the book and offering comment. Thanks to Cheri Keller Roling, Katelynn Omi Monson, Robert Clarillos, Maureen Morgan, Dennis Lynch,

Janet Moreland, (www.loveyourbigmuddy.com), and Patrick Pilla (Patrick the filmmaker/YouTube) for the use of their beautiful photography. Thank you West Valley Writers Workshop, Thursday West Valley Writer's Critique Group, Jerry Collins (www.author2market.com), and Ken Johnson (www.yourEbookBuilder.com). And, to Robert, thank you for *Everything*.

~A Blessing for Boaters~
May there be a special marina
waiting for you in the Great Beyond,
where the neighbors are quiet,
and the dogs are all good.

www.KariEJohnston.com

Bernardo
2004 to 2016
The smartest one on my boat.

An excerpt from Book 2 in the Pippi Series
Retreat to Dog Beach

Bentley. His luxurious, blonde coat billows in the wind created by the speed of his owner's yacht.

After a glorious day on the St. Croix River, the throttles are wide open. The pristine white cruiser races up the Mississippi River to its berth at the St. Paul Yacht Club.

Unattended, Bentley sits at the stern. His custom collar, designed with square, hand-milled, beads spells out his name, B E N T L E Y. Thick leather straps secured to coordinating metal hardware hold the collar together, creating a highly functional yet beautiful piece of jewelry—for show.

The sturdy, leather leash also features the dog's name with matching hardware.

267

The end of the leash, hooked solidly to a nearby cleat, prevents the purebred golden retriever from jumping overboard.

But when Canadian honkers fly overhead, Bentley's pedigree as a bird dog overrides his owner's high-brow ways. The dog's keen eyes follow the geese as they circle around the river-bottom and glide to a landing on Pigs Eye Lake.

With a eager glance toward his master for approval, he prepares to do what he does best—*retrieve*! The yacht speeds past the lake's boggy southern entrance.

Bentley jumps.

The solid hardware of the collar and leash hold, dragging the dog behind the speeding yacht. The force of the cruiser's wake shoves Bentley's head underwater. His owner, unaware that the dog is in a fight for his life, speeds up.

A link between the E and N bends and then, mercifully, breaks. The collar busts open and the dog rolls across the wake. He fights to get his bearing, coughing out river water from his long, handsome snout.

Instinct tells him to paddle . . .